If She Dares

Mikal Dawn

121
PUBLISHING HOUSE
I lift my eyes to the mountains...

Cover photos:
Front cover design by: Mikal Hermanns
Back cover design by: Teresa Tysinger, https://teresatysinger.com/
Seattle Panorama: dibrova/shutterstock.com
Desktop: Jeff Sheldon/unsplash.com
Couple: luckybusiness/depositphotos.com
Author photo: Jeffrey Conger Photography, 2016
jeffreycongerphotography.com

First edition, 121 Publishing House, 2018

ISBN-13: 978-1-7337830-0-2

Praise for *Count Me In*

"Fun and flirty, *Count Me In* is a perfect companion to your summer vacation."
- Sarah Monzon, author of *All of You*

"Mikal Dawn's debut novel is such a fun combination of tenderness, romance, and tickle-your-funnybone humor. Combine an adventure-loving hero and his sordid past with an accident-prone, feet-on-the-ground heroine and her mountain of worries, and you have a delightful romance that shows how love gives us the courage to soar beyond our insecurities. Allegra is such a likeable and relatable heroine, second-guessing herself, but working hard to help others achieve their dreams. Ty is a kind-hearted hero who's learned the value of what matters most. Don't miss out on this delightful debut!"
- Pepper Basham, author of *Just the Way You Are* and the Penned in Time series.

For Jesus. Always first. This is all because of You.

For the best husband I never could have imagined. You're my heart outside my body. I love you. Also, thanks for all the geeky fodder for this hero! Ha!

For Carol Moncado and Bethany Turner. You ladies are the bomb, and I'm so thankful for your friendship, love, and support. #MiBeCaForever

Chapter

One

*L*ia ran through the prestigious 148-year-old halls, red ponytail flying behind her.

No one had ever accused her of being calm. Or graceful.

Oomph!

Least of all the Chancellor of Rainier University.

Was it possible to melt into the floor? *Please let it be possible, Lord.* She peeked down at her toes. No sinking. Shoot. That meant she had to brave a look at Chancellor McGarville. Ten bucks said he'd be red-faced and ready to fire her on her first day as his secretary.

Lia let her gaze travel slowly from his single Monk Oxford shoes—pretty fashionable for a 76-year-old man—up the navy pinstripe pants, past the matching jacket, to the...lavender dress shirt? With the collar open and no tie? In the morning? The chancellor must be ponying up for a GQ spread or something.

Wait...her gaze had to travel further than the 5'9" man she'd met a couple of weeks earlier at her interview. Quite a bit further.

Swallowing hard, she braved those last few inches until she met piercing eyes so dark she couldn't separate the pupil from the iris.

Uh-uh. Definitely not McGarville. Unless Chancellor McGarville suddenly turned into a younger Keanu Reeves. She snickered.

"Miss Walker. You're late."

Her heart leapt in her throat. The words came from the breathtaking stranger standing only inches away, his voice—rich, luscious depth, like a baritone singing an old hymn. No, this wasn't the grey-haired chancellor whose voice had reminded her of her grandfather's and whose aftershave reminded her of, well...her grandfather's.

There was a definite similarity between this guy and the man who'd interviewed her a few weeks earlier. It was the voice. Oh, that voice. Mm. One was less impacted by the passing of time than the other, but they were both authoritative and commanding and delicious...

Uh, no. Not delicious. She didn't mean to think delicious.

"Please, come in." The man stood to the side and motioned for her to enter. So, enter she did. In a bit of a daze.

The similarities definitely stopped at the voice, and for sure didn't carry over to the scent. Nothing about her grandfather's aftershave had ever made her feel like she wanted to grab a stranger by the front of his shirt and bury her nose into his neck. Hoo boy, she didn't dare. Better bury that train of thought instead of her nose and get this meeting back on track.

"I'm sorry I'm late. Jerry, my hamster, got loose, then parking—"

"It's fine, Miss Walker. I get it. Believe me." A corner of his full lips lifted. "Well, except maybe the hamster bit. I only arrived a moment before I heard you thundering down the hall."

The relief was palpable, though her cheeks warmed. She cleared her throat. "Chancellor McGarville, I...well, I kind of remember you looking..."

His eyes widened a hot second before he burst into a laugh that matched his baritone voice. "I'm sorry," he wheezed. "You really thought I was McGarville?" He bent over at the waist, a hand stretched out to hang on to the door frame.

She rolled her eyes. "It isn't that funny."

"But you've met him. How could you think—" He belted out another laugh.

Whatever. "I didn't *actually* think you were the chancellor." Seriously, if he thought she would mistake him for the chancellor, he didn't think very highly of himself. "So, if you're not Chancellor McGarville, who in the world are you?" Lia watched as the stranger, who still hadn't introduced himself, she noticed—*rude*—walked over to the desk and sat down. She followed and sat across from him in a brown leather-tufted chair. Typical of an older, esteemed man. And it almost suited the guy across from her.

Almost.

He leaned his elbows up on the desk and rested his hands in front of him, gripped almost as if he was praying. But why would he be praying? She had no clue.

Wait... "Who are you and what have you done with the chancellor?"

"Um, well." He picked up a pen and twisted it between his fingers. "Chancellor McGarville asked me to meet you here. He had a heart attack this past weekend and won't be back to work for at least a few weeks, if not a bit longer."

A heart attack? "Will he be okay?"

The stranger waved a hand in front of him. "He will, thankfully. The old man still has a lot of life left in him. But he has to keep on the down-low for a while. Less stress, less on-the-go, you know?"

Lia nodded. She knew. "That's good. He seemed like a nice man. It's great he'll be okay." She squirmed a little, hating that she had to ask, but this was her livelihood. "So, he's reassigning me to someone else until he returns?"

The man's gaze darted around the room, the morning sun beaming in through the two windows to their right, before resting back on hers, his cheeks pink. "Uh, no. There's no one who needs a secretary right now." He set the pen down. "I'm afraid there's no work for you, Miss Walker."

Her stomach dropped. "No work? How can there be no work? This is a university. You're telling me there's *nothing* I can be doing?"

Jumping out of her chair, she glared at the man. "I quit my other job to take this one. Burned those bridges to a char." *Literally.* "I have no way to pay my bills. My rent!" Speaking of, her rent was due in three weeks. She'd been hoping that her first pay would be in her account by then to cover the small but expensive Seattle apartment.

She dropped back in her chair, bent over and grasped the sides of her head. "What am I going to do?"

The office was silent for a moment, giving her time to think. She hadn't been joking when she said she'd burned the bridges at her old job. When she was first hired on as an administrative assistant at the car dealership, all had been fine. She'd gone into work, done her job—and done it well, thanks very much—and gone home. When she'd been promoted to the general manager's assistant, she thought she'd hit gold. It was a good increase in pay, and though the hours were long to start out with, they were manageable. Then she started working later and later, until she was working with her boss past closing. It was when they'd started staying late enough that they were the last two people remaining in the building that he'd hit on her—despite his "happy" marriage—that she'd started looking for another job. When Chancellor McGarville offered her the position of his executive assistant, well... Between his hands and her fire, she was thankful for the signed agreement in her safe at home.

She lifted her gaze to the man staring at the pen in front of him. "Who are you, anyway?"

He startled, as if he'd forgotten she was even there. "Didn't I introduce myself?"

She quirked a brow. "Uh, no. Otherwise I wouldn't be asking who you are."

"Oh." He grinned and held out his hand to shake. "I'm Garrison McGarville, grandson of the famous Chancellor Theodore McGarville."

※ ※ ※

It was a very good thing the woman across from him didn't have water in her mouth. She likely would have sputtered all over him. Not that his suit was worth much, but it was the only suit he owned.

"You're Chancellor McGarville's grandson?"

"In the flesh." She seemed to have a habit of repeating him. Curious.

"And you're here to fire me before I even get truly hired." She ran slender fingers along the smooth, dark red hair leading back to her ponytail. Eyes the color of walnut wood stared off into space. "I have no job and no way to pay rent," she whispered.

He'd thought about her predicament during the quiet moment they'd just had. And he thought he had a solution. Maybe.

"You haven't even been to Human Resources to sign the paperwork, have you?"

She grimaced. Not the best look for such a pretty face, but she still made it look more than halfway good. "No. I'm seriously without a job?"

"Technically, yes." He hesitated. It was kind of an off-beat thought, but it might work, at least until Grandpa could return to the university. "But I have an idea."

Lia scooted forward on the chair, her pale cheeks regaining some color. Good. "You've thought of a job on campus?"

"Uh, not exactly. Not on campus, anyway."

"It's okay. I can work off-campus until the chancellor returns to work. As long as I have something to pay the bills." Her mouth formed a smile framing straight white teeth. His heart stuttered.

"Mr. McGarville?"

"What? Oh!" His heart must have stopped for longer than he'd thought and he'd been caught staring. *Yeah, you're a bag full of ice, you're so cool, Garr.* "Sorry," he mumbled. "The job I'm thinking of really is just temporary, but it'll probably last at least a few weeks."

"I'll take it." She smacked her hand on the desk.

Huh? "But you don't even know what it is yet. Or what it pays."

"Will it pay enough to keep me housed in Seattle for the next month or two?"

He tapped his fingers on the desk, considering her. If the pay was high enough, would she take the job? Someone really needed to do it; it couldn't be him—he'd already tried and failed. But what did he know about this woman other than Grandpa Theo thought he'd hit the jackpot when she accepted the job offer.

Well, if his grandfather liked her so much, then she would be a good choice for the job.

"It will."

"Then I'll take it."

"But don't you want to know what you'll be doing?"

"Just tell me where to go and let them know I'm coming." She picked up the bag she'd placed on the hardwood floor when she first sat in the chair, and turned that Bambi gaze on him.

"Actually, get out your car keys. You'll need to follow me."

"Follow you?"

Garrison stuck out his hand. "I'm your new boss.

Chapter

Two

This couldn't be right. Why was Garrison McGarville leading her into an apartment building? "Where do you think you're taking me?"

He pushed the button to call the elevator then turned to face her. His eyes were like the midnight sky on a moonless night. And they sparkled like they were full of stars.

Oh sheesh. She made herself nauseous with her romantic thoughts.

"The job. I'm taking you to the job."

What in the wor— She drew back her purse and whomped his chest with it, turning to run. She almost started yelling "Stranger danger!" but thought better of it. Because, y'know, she wasn't seven.

"Not *that* kind of job!" The nutty man chased after her. She could hear his feet stomping the floor as he gained on her. Why was the apartment lobby so *big*? She reached the doors and punched through onto the city street.

"Lia, wait! I swear." Cars motoring past quieted the stomping to a thud. Panting for breath—was that Garrison or her? She slowed. It was clear she needed to join a gym.

Maybe CrossFit would work for her. Or Pilates. Or just a walk around Pike Place Market.

Behind her, the stomps and thuds stopped completely. She turned to find Garrison bent at the waist, one hand on his knee, the other braced against the brick exterior of the building. She wasn't the only one who needed a good workout.

He looked up. "Organ—" he panted, "—ization." His head dropped. Another pant. "Help me."

Oh no! "Help you? Are you having a heart attack, too?" Bad hearts must run in the family. She fumbled for her phone. "I'm calling 9-1-1. Hang on." Though she really should leave him to die considering he'd just tried to accost her.

"No!" A huff of breath. "No attack."

If this wasn't a heart attack, he sure was out of shape for a slender man.

"Help with organization."

"Help with...you mean, you? You need *me* to help *you* organize?"

"My home. Yes." He stretched to his full height, getting some of his energy back. "I just moved in, but I'm what you could call, I guess, a...pack rat."

She was no organization queen herself, being late for her first day on the job a good example. But she did love a clean home with everything in its place. Well, almost everything. She couldn't talk when it came to books piled on her coffee table. And end table. And bedside table. And kitchen table. After all, tables were just a different version of a shelf, right?

And she needed the money.

She squinted her eyes at him. Could she trust him? Could she afford not to? "Let me see what you have, then I'll decide whether or not to take the job." Hopefully this wasn't some kind of lure. If he promised her books, she'd high-tail it out of there. Books were her version of candy from a windowless van.

He tilted his head back and mouthed something to the ceiling before addressing her. "Follow me."

Trotting back to the elevator, he pushed the button. They must be the only ones walking around the building right now because it opened right up, as if waiting patiently for them. He pressed number twelve, and the machine shot upward. Before she knew it, they were standing in front of apartment 1205.

He inserted a key then turned to face her. "I, uh..." Garrison shook his head, then pushed the door open and walked through, flipping a switch as he did.

The overhead light shone down on boxes. Lots of boxes. All along the short hallway...stacked to the ceiling.

"Oh. Wow." Her eyes stung, as if she'd opened them wide in the middle of a windstorm. "That's a lot of boxes."

He ducked his head. "That's not all of them."

Turning to his left, he took a step through a doorway. The kitchen. The kitchen with boxes stacked on the counters.

"Ooookay. Well, that's a few more boxes, isn't it? But doable. Now, where would you like me to start?"

"Uh, we're not done."

"Obviously. There's a lot of boxes here that need to be unpacked."

He shrugged. "Unpacked...and gone through."

She bobbed her head. "True. If you have this many boxes, you obviously have a lot of things. You weren't kidding when you said you're a packrat."

"Lia?"

She met his gaze. Why was his face so red? "Yeah?"

"There's more."

No. Way.

She swallowed. "Um...lead on."

Garrison walked past her and back into the hall where he turned left and took a few steps before turning left again. The dining and living room, one medium-sized space. Filled with boxes.

She couldn't say anything. And neither could he, obviously, because he did a 180 and walked past the hall they'd entered from and flipped another switch, shining a light on another short hall, this one with three doors—two on the left, and one on the right. He faced the first door on the left, slid a side-eyed glance at her, and entered.

She followed, which was courageous, if she did say so herself.

Inside, the small room was lined with boxes. But rejoice! They didn't go all the way to the ceiling. Just to the height of the door.

She couldn't be sure, but there may have been a small cry of distress she couldn't hold in.

The air was pregnant with silence. Garrison's chest rose with a deep breath. He led her out of the room and into the second door on the left of the hall. Another room. But lo and behold. This one had a bed in it. Actual furniture! "So, this is where you actually have a bit of space to breathe?"

He grinned. "A little. A guy needs a place to put his head at night."

Never mind that he either shared it with the opened box sitting on the bed, or he moved it around each day. Because it wasn't likely he was slowly unpacking it. There was nowhere to put anything.

"Is this the last room of boxes?"

He squeezed his eyes shut before daring a look in her direction. "There's the bathroom and laundry room."

It was a dumb question to begin with.

She stepped to the box sitting open on his bed before she glanced his way. "May I?"

"Be my guest."

Riffling through it without looking, she pulled a spongy sphere. A bouncy ball? She faced him, her lips puckering. "What in the world?"

"It's my thinking ball."

"Your thinking ball."

"My thinking ball. You know, some people put on their thinking caps. I bounce my thinking ball."

"And what do your neighbors think about that?"

"Why do you think I've moved to this place?"

She dropped the ball back in the box. "We'll get rid of that later. Your neighbors will thank me."

She reached back in the box, this time feeling around for something not so...bouncy. A-ha! She pulled on a piece of fabric and shook it out. A t-shirt—one that looked like it would fit her neighbor's six-year-old. Holding it up, she saw the back was blank. She turned to face Garrison, the edge of some white writing and what looked to be a pirate skull flashing as the shirt moved. "And this?"

"My *Goonies* shirt!"

Huh? "*Goonies*?"

His mouth dropped open. "You know. The movie. 'Never say die!'?" He plucked the shirt from her fingers and turned so she could see the front. Sure enough, *Never say die!* with skull and crossbones pictured beneath the phrase.

"Couldn't tell you. Never seen it."

Garrison fumbled the shirt, taking a step back. "No." He clutched at his chest. "No!"

The man could wail loudly.

He dropped the rag he called a keepsake to the floor and flung his arm across his forehead. "Say it isn't so!"

And was pretty dramatic. She rolled her eyes.

"You just killed a piece of my heart, Lia. You'll put me in the hospital rooming with my grandfather faster than the Sunway TaihuLight."

"Say that again?"

"The Sunway TaihuLight. It's a supercomputer in China that peaks its speed at 93.01 petaflops."

A laugh burst past her lips. "You're such a nerd."

"I prefer the term geek, thank you very much."

It figured.

⚬⚬⚬

Lia opened her mouth, likely to defend herself for never having seen the movie. Well, the woman had no excuses. Not today. "That's it. I'll order some lunch and we'll watch *Goonies* while we eat."

"Garrison?"

He picked the shirt off the floor and laid it on the bed before turning to her. "Yeah?"

"Well," her fingers drummed on her thigh. He doubted she was even aware she was doing it. "I kind of need to start working." Her face pinked. "You know, here. Because..." She rested her gaze on him, staring intently.

Was he supposed to pick up some kind of meaning behind that stare? His sister always told him he was a bit of a dunce when it came to women. And he had a feeling Lia would agree.

"Because?" If he couldn't figure it out on his own, he had no shame in asking. Until her face went from pink to deep red.

"I, uh...I need the money."

"Oh. Right. That." His excitement fizzled like butter on a hot pan. "Let's go sit and talk about that."

She grabbed her bottom lip between her teeth. "Um, sit where?"

He stepped out of the bedroom and walked the short hall to the living room, stopping in his tracks when he viewed the scene with fresh eyes. Boxes piled high everywhere, but they weren't stacked on tables or chairs, or even couches. They were stacked on the floor. Because there were no tables or chairs, or even couches.

"Off to the coffee shop down the street it is." He turned to face her. "On the clock, my treat."

"You said the magic word."

He had no clue what she was talking about—he hadn't said 'please'—but he assumed she meant it was okay.

Closing the door behind him, he nodded at a neighbor locking their own door. "Good morning."

"How do to your wife and you." The older man tipped his imaginary cap at Lia and walked off.

She gasped. "Oh, we're not—" The man turned the corner and was out of earshot. "So much for putting that thought to rest."

"It was a nice rhyme, though." The beautiful woman next to him gawked. "What? It was. 'How do to your wife and you.' How could that not be a nice rhyme?"

She mumbled something that he couldn't make out, but it sounded suspiciously like, "You're a strange man." Which he couldn't—and wouldn't—deny.

Once they reached the elevator, he walked past it and to the fire door, turning the handle to open it. "I hope you don't mind. I always take the stairs down. Just in case the elevator decides to plunge on its descent."

Did he just hear a snort come from behind him? "You do know that elevators can plunge on their ascent, too, right?"

"I prefer to be an optimist." Though his back was to her, he grinned anyway. Somehow, he knew she was holding back a laugh herself.

*C*hapter
*T*hree

*T*he process of making a latte always fascinated her. Grinding the beans, tamping them down, the rasp of the espresso machine as it frothed milk and spat hot water through to mix it with the syrups and sauces waiting in a giant mug. All for a little taste of heaven on earth.

In her mind, anyway.

She watched Garrison sip at his tea and shuddered. Tea? Really? Could he be trusted? Tea drinkers were sketchy humans, after all.

"You know, I've always been suspicious of coffee drinkers."

The languid sip of hazelnut latte choked its way down her throat. "Are you a mind reader?"

His brows furrowed. "What?"

She flicked her hand in front of her face. "Never mind." Dabbing a napkin at her lips, she sat straight in her cushy chair and faced man seated across from her. "So, the details. That's a lot of work up in your place."

"Yeah." His lips pursed. "I'll work through it with you, of course, but I kind of need you to keep me focused. And ruthless. Because, uh, as you could see, I don't have tons of furniture. No room for it." He grinned. "And I need to make room for it, or I'll forever be a bachelor." His gaze flicked down to the London Fog steaming from his cup.

Her stomach jumped, as if taking a ride in a kangaroo's pouch. She turned her mug so the handle faced to the left, then turned it again so it was perpendicular to her.

And one last turn so it was back in its original position, ready for the next sip.

She might be just a little strange, but no stranger than the man sitting across from her. He may look like an Adonis, but he had a personality more like the experimental physicist on the TV comedy she loved.

She watched as he took a sip of his tea. "I refuse to violate the prime directive and mention anything about your coffee drinking."

Case in point. She shook her head. "What are you talking about?"

He eyed her. "Prime directive. It means, 'don't interfere with underdeveloped societies.' Obviously coffee drinkers are an underdeveloped society. But I'll let you be." He reached over and patted her hand, a smirk lighting his face.

He was a brat. "I'll have you know, coffee drinkers are quite beautiful, enlightened creatures. With excellent taste."

Garrison grunted, but she was pretty sure he was more suppressing a laugh than in a state of dismay. "So, let's talk details. What do you think a job like this is worth, money-wise?"

From nerdy to uneasy. How she hated these conversations. "Well, I uh..."

"Yeah. Awkward much?"

She laughed. "Just a little."

He ran a hand over his hair, slicking it back. As soon as he let go, it sprung back into place, the sunlight filtering in through the coffee shop window making it shine. "Would you rather be paid hourly, salary, or for the project as a whole?"

"Good question." She lifted the mug to her lips and sipped. "I guess the fairest way would be for the project."

"I can deal with that." Garrison named a number that made her brows shoot up.

"Are you sure?"

"You have rent to pay, right?"

She eyed him. "Just what exactly do you do for a living that you can afford that?"

He smiled. "I'm in cybersecurity." And he left it at that.

"I didn't realize the pay was so good." He just shrugged, but since he'd been the one to offer the wage—higher than what she would have suggested—she wouldn't turn it down. "That's generous. Thank you." Lia stuck out her hand. "Deal."

Garrison enclosed her hand in his, strong fingers grasping hers. "Deal."

The money may be a deal, but what was the "deal" with the shock waves moving through her at his touch?

<hr>

Wow. Okay. That was a zing if he'd ever felt one. And judging by the wide brown eyes, she'd felt it, too.

Hm.

"We should probably head back so we can take stock." When Lia laid her napkin down, he noticed her trembling fingers. She'd had a rough day. He doubted she'd be as affected by their touch as he'd been. But in his dreams...

He stood. "Ready?"

"As ever."

Garrison led Lia back to his condo, ready to start the long process. At least, he kind of hoped it would be a long process. He rather liked being around her. She was funny and obviously intelligent. And okay, gorgeous, too.

Entering the elevator to go up to his floor, he decided to ignore her rather glum statement about the thing plummeting while it ascended. Being stuck on an elevator already gave him the creeps, but plunging to his death? No thanks. His new friend from church, Tyler Hawk, did enough of that to creep him out for life. He co-owned a local extreme outdoor adventure company and had been trying to talk him into joining them on an excursion or two for a while. His wife, Allegra, had the right idea, even if she'd been crazy enough to join her husband a few times.

"Where do you want to go?"

"Heaven."

"What?"

"You asked me where I want to go. I answered heaven. It's a reasonable desire."

"Garrison, I asked you where you want to start. Not go."

"No, I heard you ask where I want to go."

"You heard wrong, buddy."

He snorted. "Buddy?"

"At least you heard right that time."

"I think you're smoking something."

He was saved from her reply when the doors slid open. Stepping off the elevator, he called over his shoulder. "We should probably start in the living room to make room for some furniture. But I still want to go to heaven."

She was silent a moment before responding. "Yeah, okay. That's reasonable."

Chapter Four

They walked through his door and entered the living room, where he wanted to start organizing. Looking around at the boxes, she didn't know how they were going to accomplish it in only two weeks. She sucked in her cheeks and chewed. "We might need to go buy some shelving before we start just so we have somewhere to place the things you want to keep. At least until we can find a permanent spot for them."

"Yeah." Garrison turned his head, gaze searching the room. "That's probably a good idea. I also want a cabinet or two with glass doors. I, uh...have a lot of board games I want easy access to."

Board games? The man was turning totally geeky on her. In a very cute way. "We can do that. For the shelving, do you have an idea of what you like, style-wise?"

"Uhh..."

That's what she thought. "And that's what Pinterest is for."

"Pinterest?"

"Please tell me you've heard of it."

Garrison started whistling, trying to act all innocent—as if that were even possible. She smirked at the attempt, as she simultaneously felt giddiness bubble up inside of her, like a child who'd just been told they could have some cotton candy. Another person she could pull into a Pinterest addiction. It was good to not be alone in her obsession.

Twenty minutes later, Garrison's breathless voice whispered beside her as they stood at the bar-height counter between his kitchen and living room, scrolling through the app on his phone. "You can find all that on Pinterest?"

She laughed. "Yep." She'd created an account for him, and before she knew it, he had twelve "boards" for everything from games to furniture to his favorite b-list actors. The man was in virtual heaven. He did say he wanted to go to heaven, didn't he?

"Well, I think I know what I want." He pointed a finger to an off-white, four-shelf cabinet with framed glass doors. "What do you think?"

She clicked on the tab for the specs and read the measurements. At five feet, nine inches, she wasn't short. And this cabinet would come up to her eyes. "Isn't that a little big?" She stood and held her hand at eye-level. "It will be about this tall."

Garrison ducked his head, color creeping up the back of his neck. "Actually, it might not be big enough."

"But isn't this for your board games?"

"Yeah." He shrugged. "I have quite a few."

She narrowed her eyes. "How many is 'quite a few'?"

He pulled at the collar of his shirt. "Uh."

Lia watched as he walked into the hall where at least a dozen—maybe even two dozen—boxes were stacked then turned to face her.

She stared at him.

He stared back.

Silence.

"No." He couldn't be inferring what she thought he was trying to infer. No. Stinkin'. Way.

He grinned, looking like a dark-haired Dennis the Menace.

"I quit."

"Think of it this way," he said. "This part will go quick. I mean, it's just unpacking and putting them into a cabinet. Then voila!" His arms shot up toward the ceiling. "A cleared hall."

Lia shook her head. He couldn't think this would be easy. And that cabinet he thought would be big enough? No. Wouldn't even be close. "There have to be at least a hundred games in those boxes."

"Somewhere between one hundred and...three hundred."

She shook her head. "I should have asked for medical with this job. I'm likely to get a hernia."

"You're up for this." His face took on a sly grin. "Come on. I dare you."

He was an infuriating, adorable man-child for daring her. She huffed. "Fine. But we're going to need a bigger game cabinet."

He wouldn't blame her if she wanted to quit. He had a *lot* of boxes to comb through. Hm. Maybe he should offer medical.

"Okay. So, if you think that cabinet will be too small, what do you suggest?"

Lia stepped forward and grabbed a box. "Let's see about how big these things are." She ripped off the tape that sealed the top, opened the flaps, and pulled out a game. Then another, and another. Four bigger boxed games and a few small card games later, she spoke. "Are all your boxes like this? A mix of sizes?"

What was the right answer here? "Yes?"

Her gaze flicked up to meet his. "Are you asking *me*?"

"No. I just really don't know for sure. But we can always buy two of those cabinets."

"Dude." Did she seriously just call him dude? "I really don't think even two will hold all these." She glanced down at the watch on her slim wrist. "Traffic shouldn't be terrible by now. Let's go."

"Go? Where are we going?"

"To my favorite store."

"Are you Target-obsessed like all the other women I know? Is that where we're going?"

She grinned, her wide smile brightening the apartment. "I am. But no, that's not where we're going. We're heading to my other obsession. A beautifully big, blue and yellow Swedish store." She grabbed his hand, her skin warming his. "Come on, buddy. Time to grow you up with some big-boy furniture."

"I don't wanna grow up!"

Her laugh floated back to him as he followed, its musical tones sending shockwaves throughout his body.

Making their way from downtown Seattle to Renton, normally a twenty-five-minute drive, took just over an hour due to an accident on the I-5. But they made it. And entered the huge box, rode the escalator to the top level, and began following the lit arrows to the living room storage area.

"Are you a looker?"

He snapped his head in her direction. "I'd like to think I'm not terrible looking."

Lia rolled her eyes, but the shading of her cheeks sent a jolt of electricity through his veins. "I meant, do you like to take your time and really look at things, or do you make quick decisions?"

"I like to look but I'm a decisive guy, not one who'll stand here and debate for two hours over which cabinet to get. If I see something I like, I'll stop looking."

She lifted one eyebrow, as if she didn't believe him. "Uh-huh."

They stopped in front of a section of cabinets, ranging from shorter to chin-height, but none of them caught his eye. "Nothing here."

"What? We just got here. You haven't even looked."

"I told you, I might be a 'looker,' but I'm fast. And hungry. Want to grab some Swedish meatballs while we're here?"

"Garrison McGarville, not until you choose something to store all those games. We aren't walking out of here empty-handed."

She was a bossy little thing. He liked it. "Yes Ma'am." Sudden pain radiated down his arm. "Did you just *pull* my *arm hair?*"

The smug look on her face was answer enough, but she opened her mouth anyway. "I sure did."

It was in that moment that, despite only knowing her a few hours, he knew he'd fallen in love.

$\mathscr{C}$hapter $\mathscr{F}$ive

$\mathscr{J}$t took a little more than twenty minutes, but Garrison was true to his word. He'd chosen four tall, white and glass cabinets that stood almost to door-height. Lia grabbed the tags detailing where to find the cabinets in the warehouse on the lower floor then snatched Garrison's hand. "I'm famished. Ever since you mentioned Swedish meatballs, my mouth has been watering."

"Yeah," he growled with a look in her direction. "I know what you mean."

"Oh, come on. That wasn't so painful, right?"

"Not until I check out and pay for it."

She couldn't tell if he was joking or not. Was he regretting his decision to hire her? But he really did need furniture. And he was no doubt right that taking care of the games would be the easiest place to start.

"Garrison?" She slowed her steps as they entered the cafeteria.

"Yeah?" His hungry eyes devoured...the menu. Not her, the menu.

She sighed. She'd just met him a matter of hours ago. She couldn't expect a practical stranger to want to take her in his arms and kiss the daylights out of her. Especially in the middle of a Swedish big-box store.

She really had to get her head in the game and off the man standing just in front of her. "Are you sure about those cabinets? If they're too much, we can always go to a thrift store and find something I can make over for you instead."

Lia watched as his hand drifted to his flat stomach and he rubbed in a circular motion. "It's good," he absently replied. Had he even really heard her?

"Are you positive?"

"Uh-huh." He took another step forward. "Should I get the mashed potatoes or fries?"

He definitely wasn't listening to her.

"If I get the mashed potatoes, I can get more gravy. But if I get the fries, I can always ask for more gravy, right?" He mumbled under his breath and left her side to pick up a tray. The man might be more interested in food than Scooby was in Scooby-Snacks.

She followed in his footsteps, matching his meatballs and fries and upping him on the gravy. It *was* good gravy, after all.

The moment Garrison shoved a gravy-covered meatball in his mouth, he closed his eyes and chewed slowly. No, it wasn't gourmet. And yes, there were other foods out there that were far more delectable. But he still loved it.

Lia set down her tray across from him, shook out a napkin and laid it on her lap. After a sip of her water, she picked up her fork and sliced a meatball in half.

The woman sitting across from him was a walking contradiction. She ate her food with such daintiness, but he didn't know if he'd met a less graceful person.

"I dare you to stuff a whole meatball in your mouth."

Her fork stopped halfway to her mouth, her wide eyes focused on him. "What?"

"Go on," he waved a fry in her direction. "Take a whole meatball and stuff it in your mouth. They aren't even big."

Her face scrunched up, creating faint lines beside her eyes. "They're big enough."

"C'mon. I dare you."

She stared, her lips twitching. "Are we in second grade?"

Lia's gaze followed the movement of his fry. Hm. He moved it closer to his lips. Her eyes kept following. He opened his mouth and watched as she swallowed.

And he stuffed the entire fry, dripping with gravy, in and chomped down. So good.

Lia rolled her eyes.

"Your turn. I'm up to double-dog daring you."

"Fine," she huffed. A second later, she stabbed a full meatball with her fork and shoved it in her mouth. He laughed as her cheeks puffed out while she chewed.

Once she swallowed, she glared at him. "I swear you're a ten-year-old boy stuck in a grown man's body."

He raised his water glass. "To that ten-year-old boy."

Lia laughed. "So, what happened to the furniture from your last apartment? Where did you move from?"

"I just moved into this apartment from an extended-stay hotel."

Her fork paused in mid-air on its way to her mouth, a fry at the end of it. Who ate fries with a fork, anyway?

"Why were you in an extended-stay hotel?"

"I came back from working overseas a month ago."

"Overseas? Where overseas? What were you doing there?"

He laughed. "Are you sure you're not a journalist? You ask a lot of questions."

Lia set her fork on her plate, grabbed her cup and raised it to her lips. "Not a journalist, just curious." She sipped.

He watched as she tilted her head back a bit, exposing the length of her neck. It bobbed as she swallowed the water. Fascinating. She was fascinating.

And he was creepy for staring. He cleared his throat. "Uh, I was in Berlin, working in IT Security for the U.S. Embassy."

"Oh wow. That had to be incredible."

"I loved living there. It was an easy drive to so many places in Europe."

"Uh...why in the world are you back here then?" Her mouth formed a small O. "Were you fired?" she whispered.

Garrison laughed. "No, I wasn't fired. I missed my grandpa so started looking at other government service jobs out here and found one that paid even better since I was able to gain a couple of steps—stages of a government pay scale. I'm now working in cyber security down in Tacoma at the Defense Health Agency."

She stared at him, her eyes shiny. "That's so sweet."

"That I work in cyber security? I don't know how sweet that is. Unless you mean sweet as in cool."

Lia's head shook. "No, I mean sweet that you wanted to be near the Chancellor so you came home. Were you raised here?"

"Nah. I was born in San Diego and lived there until I went to college for my bachelor's at Boston University. After that, I went to Scotland for my master's degree, and from there over to Germany. I was really lucky to get picked up for that one. It's really competitive. But God had a plan. And now look—here I am."

"Wow. I can say I've been to Oregon." The smirk on her face was too adorable.

Adorable? Wow. He was getting cheesy. Moving on. "How about you?"

"Seattle-born and -raised. I even attended Rainier University." She leaned forward and lowered her voice to a conspiratorial tone. "I don't get out much."

He was pretty sure everyone in the cafeteria turned to look when he let out a guffaw. But he didn't care. This woman made him laugh like no other.

Chapter

Six

Seeing the man in front of her laugh with abandon made her stomach do flips. It was ridiculous, really. People did not fall in love within hours of meeting one another. She'd never been one to believe in love at first sight, and that hadn't changed.

But like at first sight? Yeah. That she could do.

And she had.

From within her purse, Lia's phone chimed. Shoot.

"What was that?"

She bent over to dig through the bag and find her cell. "My alarm. I have a dentist appointment. We need to leave so I'm not late."

"Meh, who needs clean teeth?"

"Well, me for one. Call me crazy, but I love a good, clean tooth."

"Crazy."

Her giggle bubbled up and trickled over into the open air of the cafeteria. "That I am."

Garrison pushed back from the table and stood, gathering their trays and taking them to the tray shelves in an alcove. Once he was back, Lia slid the cabinet ticket out of her pocket and threw her bag over her shoulder. "Let's go get these babies and get back to the city."

"Sounds good to me."

A couple of minutes later, they walked into the warehouse. Lia peered up at the red and white number signs. "The tag says they're in this aisle," she pointed to the number on the paper. "We should probably get a cart."

"Be right back."

It was heavy work getting the large boxes off the shelves, and she had to admit, she wasn't much help. Her relief was palpable when a couple walked down the aisle and the man offered to help Garrison get the boxes on the cart. And her relief was even more palpable when an employee offered to help Garrison out to his car and get the boxes in the back. Thankfully, the man drove a larger SUV. It took some maneuvering, but they were able to fit them in like a puzzle.

"Does your building have a dolly to help us in with those?"

"Huh. Good question. I guess we'll find out." He turned the key in the ignition and began their trek back into Seattle. "Thanks for today. I had fun."

She grinned. "Think of all the fun we'll have tomorrow when I come back and we start unpacking. And," she glanced at his profile, enjoying the upward quirk of his lips, "purging."

Garrison groaned. "I don't like that word."

"Oh, but you will, my friend. You will."

He smiled. "I don't know if I'll be able to get these put together by tomorrow. It might be a two-man job. Er, a one-man and one-woman job, that is."

"That's okay," she shrugged. "We can do it tomorrow. It shouldn't take more than an hour."

"Famous last words, Lia." He glanced at her, his brow lifted. "You're absolutely sure you want to take on this job?"

"You dared me to. But...do you have any more 'thinking balls'?"

"Not a one," he laughed.

"Then we're good."

⁓⧐⁓

Garrison watched Lia drive off, wishing with all his might that she was staying and having dinner with him. Maybe he should have asked her out. Maybe he should have proposed.

Okay, that might be taking it too far considering their first meeting ever happened at just eight o'clock that morning.

A bus's brakes squealed down the street, jerking him out of his thoughts. The tall buildings surrounding him blocked out a lot of the sunlight, but if he looked straight up, the sky above was clear, with a few seagulls circling overhead. Maybe he could call Ty and see if he wanted a guy's night out.

He strode back into his building straight to the elevator. Lia's words from earlier that day, however, were still with him. There was no way he wanted to risk plunging to his death during an ascent to his floor. Not when she was coming back tomorrow.

Garrison turned to the stairs instead. Twelve flights of stairs weren't exactly on his to-do list today, but after running out of breath chasing Lia down this morning, he needed to do something to get back into shape. That was a highly embarrassing moment.

Much huffing, puffing, and many pauses later, he climbed the last step and entered his apartment. Now that he was looking at it through Lia's eyes, he could understand her dismay. He didn't even know how he'd amassed all this stuff and why his mother hadn't thrown it all out when he went straight to Germany after graduating with his masters in Scotland.

He pulled his cell out of his pocket and tapped on a picture of his friend from church. Ty was a newlywed, but even he had to want a guy's night every now and then.

"Hello?" He hadn't even heard the line ring.

"Hey Ty, it's Garr. How are you?"

"Great man. It's good to hear from you. What's up?"

"I know it's short notice, but I was wondering what you're up to tonight? If you wanted to grab dinner or go do something."

"Ah, man. I'm sorry. Allie just made us dinner. We're eating early because she's heading out with a friend of hers for a girl's night. I was gonna go to the gym, though. I know it probably wasn't what you were thinking, but you want to join me there?"

A gym. Well, he *had* just been thinking he needed to get back into shape. "Sure, where at?"

He wrote down the details and agreed to meet Tyler there in an hour. They'd met at church on Garrison's first Sunday back in the States and had hit it off immediately. Later that week, they'd found themselves at the same Bible study, and that sealed the deal. A friendship was born.

A friendship that was apparently going to take him to the gym. He sighed and went to his room to change.

Metal clanging on metal, grunts on top of grunts. It was a gun show inside the gym. And he was pretty sure he'd never felt more inadequate than he did at that moment. Because let's be honest, he was a government worker, and while the government encouraged physical fitness, he sat behind a computer all day. And then his geeky tendencies kept him behind a computer—or in front of a board game—at night. A gym wasn't his regular hangout.

Tyler Hawk had every intention of changing that.

Speaking of Ty... Garrison looked around the gym until he spotted the tall, muscular blond. Yeah. Just what he needed: to spend an evening in a gym beside a former NFL tight end.

His feelings of inadequacy took a further nosedive.

Tyler lowered the shoulder press, wiped his face with a gray towel, and looked over at Garrison. He stood and wandered over to him, stopping along the way to say hi to another guy.

"Hey man," Tyler grabbed Garrison's hand and pumped it once. "Thanks for meeting me here. It's been a couple of days since I was able to work out."

"Yeah, uh...me too." He didn't meet Tyler's gaze. No doubt he would see the lie in Garrison's eyes. "Already started?" Good. That would mean less time in the gym to embarrass himself.

"Nah, I was just warming up." Warming up by doing a shoulder press? Sure. "Want to start with a run on the track?"

It was now or never. "Yup."

He tried to pace Tyler, he really did. But it was useless. Within seconds, Ty was way ahead of him, eventually lapping him. But Garrison kept his chin up. He wasn't a runner—that was obvious by his attempt at chasing Lia down that morning—but once they started in on the weights, it wouldn't be that bad.

Right?

Chapter

Seven

"Are you decent?" Lia sure hoped so, because she was standing in Garrison's entry hall, ready to work. Before she'd left yesterday, he'd given her the key to his building, and a key to his apartment, insisting she use it since she'd be here every day working.

"Just a sec," his rich voice called out.

She wasn't sure if it was her or just a noise from the bedroom, but she thought she heard a low hum. And a thump, too. Wow, her heart was loud. She'd felt it bumping against her chest, the thought of seeing Garrison again making her giddier than if Wile E. Coyote had caught the Roadrunner.

Thump.

Maybe it wasn't thumping out of giddiness. Maybe she should see a doctor.

Thump, thump.

Okay, this was getting serious. If she asked, maybe Garrison would drive her to the hospital. She felt fine, but—

"Garrison?" Her eyebrows shot up as he rounded the corner, hanging for dear life onto crutches. "What happened?"

Pink climbed up his neck and colored his cheeks. "I, uh...dropped a weight on my foot."

"What? A weight?"

"Yeah. I was at the gym last night with a friend and lost my grip. Gave myself a pretty bad bruised foot. The crutches are only for comfort. At least, the doc said they'd be more comfortable than walking on a bruised foot. I don't believe him."

"Oh no! How are you feeling? Do you need anything? Ice?"

"Actually, ice would be good, but I can get it."

"Aren't you supposed to be sitting down with your foot up?"

"Well yeah, but..."

'But' indeed. Where would he sit? The best he could do was lay down on his bed, because without any furniture... "Okay. I need to go shopping for you again. For a couch and table or ottoman. Something you can sit and rest your foot on." She eyed him. "If I send you back to bed, do you trust me to pick out a couch for you?"

Garrison rubbed a hand down his face. "I do. I'm still tired. We thought it might be broken, so we headed to the ER and were there until almost midnight, and I didn't sleep very well."

Lia moved around him and walked back to his bedroom. The covers were still thrown back, so she plumped his pillow, turned to face him, and pointed her finger at the mattress. "Get back in there. I'll grab you some water and, well, whatever you have to eat in that kitchen, and bring it back in here for you. Do you want anything to read?"

"Are you willing to go through the boxes to find me something to read right now?"

She grimaced. "Point taken." She dug in her shoulder bag and pulled out an eReader. "Here, there are a couple thousand books on there in every genre imaginable." She tilted her head toward the bed. "Get in there and I'll grab your food then go find a couch I can have delivered today."

A chime rang on Garrison's phone. "Someone is buzzing into the building. I don't know who, though. Hold on." He picked up his phone and swiped. "Hello?" He paused. "You didn't have to, but thanks. Come on up."

Garrison ended the call and looked up. "It's the friend I was with last night. Ty. He brought breakfast." He grinned. "If this is how people treat me when I get hurt, I need to do this more often."

"Preferably not, thanks. Because I'm now down one helper with those boxes."

He winced. "I'm really sorry. I can at least sit there and unload while you put things away, though."

"Purge them. And again, what would you sit on?"

His mouth worked like he wanted to stick his tongue out at her. "Purge. And yeah. Point taken. Again."

The knock at the door moved her to let this Ty person in. She wasn't expected the man standing in front of her, though.

"You're Tyler Hawk."

"I am," he said, lifting his hand and holding it out to shake. "And you are?" His head tiled to the side, curiosity reflecting in his eyes.

"Oh! I'm Lia Walker, Garrison's personal organizer." She took his hand and shook, the firmness of his grip startling her. She was actually shaking Tyler Hawk's hand!

"Garr told me about you last night. Between you and me, it's about time he got someone to organize his life. The guy has been living out of a suitcase for too long."

She stepped back and to the side, letting the large man in. And that's when she saw a dark-haired woman standing behind him. "Oh! I'm so sorry, I didn't see you there."

Music tinkled from her mouth in the form of laughter. "No one ever does when they first meet Ty. And that's okay." The woman's gaze lit up when she looked at Tyler. "The man has a commanding presence."

"Allie," he growled. "You're embarrassing me on purpose."

"I am," she replied, her voice a sing-song.

Lia watched as Tyler grabbed this Allie woman by the waist and kissed her soundly on the lips. One day someone would kiss her like their life depended on it. She hoped and prayed.

A throat cleared from behind Lia. "You guys. Really?"

Tyler grinned against Allie's lips. "Really."

They pulled apart, Allie's face red. She smacked Tyler's arm and turned to face Lia. "I am so sorry about that. The man doesn't have good manners."

"My mom would be offended." Ty grinned.

"By your lack of good manners."

"Admit it, you love me."

"That I do, you big lug." Allie winked at Lia. "By the way, I'm Allegra, Tyler's wife."

"It's nice to meet you." She leaned forward and gave Allegra a quick hug. After all, once you've witnessed a couple kiss like that, you were practically best friends, right?" "I'm Lia Walker."

Allie turned to Garrison, eyeing the crutches he leaned on. "Ty told me what happened. I'm so sorry."

"It's okay," he shrugged. "I need to become more familiar with the gym, it seems."

"In a week or two. Give your foot time to heal. In the meantime, however, we need to find you a couch to sit on so you don't need to spend that time in bed." Lia stepped away from the door to let the couple in.

"A couch?" Allegra turned to Garrison. "You don't have a couch?"

He was cute when his face flushed. "No."

"He was in a long-term hotel when he returned from Germany, babe. No furniture to be had."

"I was just about to get him some food and water then go shopping."

"We actually brought food." Tyler lifted a hand clutching a bag from Café Argento. "Bagels."

"We also brought tea," Allegra grimaced, "and coffee. Always coffee." She held up a cup that wafted the scent of roasted beans. Lia could really like this woman. "You're going shopping for a couch? I love shopping."

"Really?" She didn't know Allie, but she seemed like such a fun woman. "I'd love some company if you aren't busy."

Tyler grinned. "I'll stay here with Garr. Talk him through the finer points of weight lifting."

Lia laughed. "That's probably a great idea."

"Thanks, guys," Garrison deadpanned.

"Garrison?" She held out her hand. "I'll need your credit card."

Chapter Eight

"So, when did you meet?"

Garrison closed the door behind Lia and Allegra. "When did who meet?"

"You and Lia."

"Yesterday. She was late for her first day as my grandfather's secretary."

"Wait, your grandpa is back to work already?" Tyler moved into the kitchen, grabbed a glass, and poured himself some water.

"Nah. He's at home now but still recovering. He won't be back at work for a while yet. But Lia didn't know that, and Grandpa didn't have her number handy. He didn't want to call the office for it either, something about too much sympathy. He asked me to meet her and let her know what happened."

"How'd she end up here, working for you?"

Garrison told his friend the story. "I don't know how this'll work out, but it has to be better than how I'm living now, right?"

Tyler moved his gaze around the kitchen and over the bar counter into the living room. "Yeah, for sure. So, man," he moved his gaze to meet Garr's, "when are you going to ask her out?"

"How about never?" He turned, using his crutches to move back to his room, the only place he could sit. His foot was killing him.

"And why not?" Of course Tyler would follow him.

He reached his bed, leaned his crutches against the footboard, and used his mattress for stability while he sat and squirmed to make himself comfortable. "I just met her, for one."

"And? People who just meet go on dates all the time. It doesn't mean you have to marry her."

His stomach flipped. Marriage? He wiped at the sweat that broke out on his forehead at the thought of a lifetime commitment. "Who said anything about marriage?"

Tyler lifted his hands, palms out. "Whoa, I was just saying it *doesn't* mean marriage." He scratched at his chin. "Though you two make a good-looking couple."

Garrison threw a pillow at Tyler's face, only to hear him laughing as he caught it. "Don't you have somewhere to be? Work, maybe?"

"Nope. Story has the shop covered. And there are no excursions today." Hawk's Flight Outdoor Adventures was Tyler's post-NFL career. The man thrived on extreme outdoor sports. Allegra didn't. Garrison was still confused over how those two ended up together, but he supposed you couldn't help who you loved.

"You know," Ty continued, "we should go on a double-date."

"We should?"

"Dinner?"

"I told you, Ty. I just met Lia. She's fun and I like her, but I'd rather know more about her before I go asking her out. Besides, she's my employee. My *new* employee. What if she thinks I only hired her because I wanted to ask her out? Couldn't that be some kind of sexual harassment?"

"I think you're going a bit far, but I get where you're coming from. How about this? Let her work with you for a week or two, get to know her, then ask her out for dinner with me and Allie. In the meantime, I'll get us a reservation for—" he looked down at his smartwatch and tapped the screen— "two weeks from today. Ask her out before then."

"And if she says no?"

Tyler grinned. "She won't."

"You know it isn't *you* asking her out, right? You may not hear no, but I sure do."

"You just haven't asked the right woman before. She's the right one." Tyler shoved his shoulder. "Lay down a bit, you're looking pale. I'll go out to the living room and unpack a box."

"I wouldn't if I were you. You might find a squishy ball."

"What?"

"Never mind. But don't worry about unpacking any boxes. There's nowhere to put anything. And nowhere for you to sit out there. You can hang in here."

Tyler opened his mouth, as if to say something, when his phone started playing music.

"*Wipe Out*? An ode to the time you flipped out of the raft on the river?" He smirked.

His friend shot him a glare as he swiped his phone. "Hello?" He listened for a moment. "Shoot. Thanks, Story. I'll be there in fifteen or twenty." He tapped the screen.

"Problems?"

"Not a big one, but it's something I need to deal with myself. Will you be okay if I take off? I can come back when I'm done."

"No problem. I'm kind of tired anyway." He moved to get off the bed.

"Don't. I can see myself out. But I'll grab that tea and bagel and bring it back in here before I go. Do you need anything else? I feel guilty about your foot."

Garrison laughed. "It wasn't your fault at all. But thanks."

Tyler brought the food to him and took off, leaving Garrison in the silence of the apartment. Even in the city, it was quiet up on the twelfth floor unless he opened his windows.

He finished the bagel and laid down, grabbing Lia's eReader on the way. If he was going to be in bed for a while, it was a good opportunity to get lost in a book.

Chapter

Nine

*O*oh, look at that one." Lia turned and slid her gaze along the path Allegra's finger pointed. A crib?

"That's cute, but I don't think it's Garrison's taste." She grinned. "Though I admit I haven't known him long."

Allegra laughed. "Sorry. I'm obviously distracted." She rolled her eyes. "Back to the sofas."

They wandered among the couches until Lia saw a smoke-gray L-shaped sofa. "This one. It's perfect."

"I like that. It seems like it would suit Garrison."

Lia whipped out a measuring tape, figured the dimensions, and nodded. "Now to see if we can get this to his place today."

She found a salesperson and, after a call to the warehouse, found out they'd had a delivery rescheduled and had a slot open to deliver within two hours. "We'll take it." She held out the credit card.

With the transaction completed, she realized they had a little time to kill before they absolutely had to be back at Garrison's. "Would you like to get some coffee?"

Allie stopped walking and turned to face Lia, her hand reaching out to touch her arm. "Lia, I like you."

Laughter bubbled up. "I like you too. I take it that's a yes?"

Her newfound friend sighed. "Coffee is life. Glorious, tasty life. And I love it. I love it so hard." Her eyes slid closed. "The roasted nectar of the beans, the hot, frothy mess of milk, the sweet glory of the syrups, all turned into one beautiful, very, very large cup of heaven."

The bubbled-up laughter burst from Lia's lips. "Oh," she wiped at her eyes, "you do take it seriously, don't you?"

Allegra grinned. "You have no idea."

"Then let's go."

They left the furniture shop, hopped into Lia's older, red Corolla, and drove to the nearest coffeehouse where Allegra introduced her to the Kit Kat latte. She took a sip of Allie's and licked her lips. "That is sooo good. Wow."

"Right? Tyler just doesn't understand. He likes it, but says it isn't anything special. It's a wonder I married the man."

"It must be true love."

"Tell me about it."

Lia lifted her own hazelnut latte to her lips. "How long have you been married?"

And that was all it took to get Allegra telling the story of their run-in at a coffeehouse and how Tyler had practically forced her into some extreme outdoor sports.

"You're kidding me, right? How could he do that?"

"I needed the job. And," she leaned closer so Lia could hear her whisper, "he has the most amazing green eyes." She giggled, a blush staining her cheeks. "We've been married almost seven months."

That explained it. They were still in the honeymoon stage. Lia's parents were still married, but she couldn't remember ever seeing them act like such newlyweds. She was sure they loved each other, but she didn't know if it was real love, or more just out of habit. Sometimes she wondered. It was part of the reason she was holding out a little longer than her parents wished on dating and marriage. She wanted to be sure she got the kind of relationship Tyler and Allegra had but wanted assurance it would last like that.

High standards. Her parents even called it unrealistic, and maybe they were right. But she had faith that God would bring about the right guy in His perfect time.

She just wished His perfect time matched hers.

"We should get back to Garrison's. I'll need to clear the boxes out of the entry for the delivery guys to be able to bring in the couch."

"Oh, that's right. Let's go."

They gathered their cups, tossed them in the trash, and waved goodbye to the barista. Lia slid behind the steering wheel and pulled into the street.

"You know, we should go on a double-date."

"We what?"

"You, Garrison, me and Tyler. It would be such fun."

"You know Garrison and I aren't a couple, right? We just met yesterday."

"Semantics," Allie flipped her hand. "We would have a blast. Maybe dinner and a walk. Oh! Even better, dinner and one of the touring Broadway shows. *Cats* is opening in a couple of weeks. I've wanted to see that for a while."

"I'm not asking him out, Allie."

"Dare you."

"What is it with you people and your dares?"

"Huh?"

"Never mind. I won't ask him out, not even on a dare." Lia stuck her tongue out the side of her mouth. Childish? Yes. But it caused Allie to snicker.

She slid a glance in Lia's direction. "I'm pretty sure we're going to end up on a double-date. And I'm pretty sure you won't be the one doing the asking. That is all."

"No way, no how."

"Hm."

"Where are we going to stack these boxes, Lia?"

That was the question of the year. Garrison's home was literally out of space. She hadn't put the cabinets together yet—that was something she and Garrison were supposed to do that morning, but his foot waylaid those plans. "Hey Garr?"

His voice answered from down the hall. "Yeah?"

"Does your building have any storage you can use for a couple of days?"

Silence, then, "I actually don't know. I can call the on-site caretaker and ask."

"Thanks."

While she waited for the answer, Lia started moving some of the boxes from the closer side of the living room where the couch would go to the opposite side. It wasn't a big space, but she could put her Tetris experience to use.

Garrison appeared behind her as she set a box on a tower of other boxes. "Bad news. There isn't any storage space. I'm sorry." He pushed his fingers through his espresso-brown hair.

"It's okay, really. I think I found a way to at least get your couch in here when they arrive, which should be in—" she checked the time on her phone— "another ten minutes."

"I'm sorry Ty hasn't made it back yet. I don't know what's keeping him." Allegra reached for her phone.

"Don't worry. Honest. It really wasn't a big deal to move these around. Just took a little thinking."

"Did it hurt? The thinking?" A deep snort followed the rich voice.

Lia paused. If she pushed Garrison over, would he injure his other foot? She'd prefer to injure his mouth instead. She glared at him.

He chuckled. "I was kidding, honest!"

She took a step toward him.

"Uncle! I cry uncle!"

Another step.

"I'll make it up to you. Have dinner with me."

That got her to stop in her tracks. "Dinner?"

She wondered if his eyes could get any bigger. So, he'd said that without thinking.

"Uh, a business dinner. To talk about all this." He motioned around the apartment with his chin.

Oh. *Business* dinner. Fine. It might be worth it to go to dinner and make him pay. She'd order the most expensive item on the menu. "Okay."

Behind her, she heard Allegra mumble. It sounded like she'd said, "Told you so," but she was wrong. Garrison himself said it would be a business dinner.

Definitely not a date.

Chapter

Ten

He had to admit, the dark gray—Lia had called it "smoke gray"—looked good. The clean lines of the sofa with no ornamentation suited him. And it was comfortable. Especially the L part of the L-shape. His foot wasn't throbbing so much, now that it was raised.

"I'm lost." Lia frowned at the assembly instructions for the bookcase.

"Have a hard time reading pictures?"

If the glare coming from her was any indication, she didn't think he was very funny. He disagreed.

"Have you ever seen the instructions parody memes online for these?"

"No."

A very succinct, pointed answer. She needed more humor in her life. "You look like one."

Wow. Tough crowd. All he got was yet another glare.

"I'm holding you to that dinner. And be forewarned: it's going to be the biggest, baddest, most expensive dinner bill ever."

His heart jumped in his chest. Dare he admit the thought made him happy? Not the bill. That freaked him out worse than the horror movie scene he'd turned on one night when he'd snuck downstairs to watch TV as a kid—clowns still made him nervous—but the fact she was going to hold him to dinner. A date. They were going on a date.

"I'm with you, Lia. And I think I have the perfect restaurant in mind."

He listened to the two women talk as he went through a box Lia had brought to him earlier. There was no reason he couldn't sit on the couch and sort through his things. Lia had given him "keep," "throw out," and "give away" piles to sort into. The "give away" pile had two items in it, the "throw out" pile had nothing, and the "keep" pile had, well...he eyed the stack. A lot. That pile had a lot.

He was doing pretty good. Whomever picked up the two Archie comic books was going to be blessed indeed.

"I swear these instructions are in a completely different language. You need a degree in hieroglyphics." Lia huffed. Who knew building these bookcases would be such a test in the basic understanding of pictures?

"Look on the bright side," Allegra said, standing and stretching her arms to the ceiling, "we're one-quarter of the way there."

She slid a glare to her friend. "One-quarter of the way done building the *first of four* bookcases."

"But once we know how to build one, the rest should be as easy as a walk in the park."

Lia narrowed her gaze at Allegra. "You're an optimist, aren't you?"

"The one and only." She batted her eyelashes. "And you looooove me."

She giggled. "Wow." She didn't think she'd laughed so much and so hard in the past few months in total as she had the last two days since meeting Garrison. It was good for her soul. Not to mention the workout her belly was getting.

Garr's phone chimed, alerting him to someone at the building door wanting in. "Hello?"

"Hey man, it's Tyler."

"Come on up." He tapped the button that would open the building door for him.

In minutes, Tyler was in the living room, shuffling boxes around like they were feathers in order to give them more room to work. Seriously, the man was a machine.

And she kind of felt badly for Garrison. He sat on the new couch watching them, his gaze going back and forth between Tyler and Allegra, listening to their banter. He almost looked...lonely.

She moved to sit beside him. "Can I get you anything?"

He shook his head. "Thanks, but I'm good. I just wish I could help."

"You have at least a week before you can do that." She punched his arm. "Are you sure I can't get you anything?"

"Another box?"

"On it." She stood, stepped around the ottoman his foot was resting on, and froze. "That's a great throw out pile." She pointed at the tall stack.

"It's my keep pile."

"No."

"No?"

The man was dense. "The whole point of purging is to get rid of things. Not put them into a keep pile. That," she pointed at the offending stack of items, "should not be that large. At all."

"But I like all that."

He sounded like a petulant little boy. She threw her head back and studied the ceiling. How could she make him understand? If he didn't resolve his packrat-ish ways, he would never have a comfortable home to live in. "Garrison." She didn't mean to sound like she was patronizing him, but seriously. "You have nowhere to put anything. And even with the furniture, you still have too much stuff. Stuff that, let's be honest, isn't necessary to your well-being."

Garrison's shoulders lifted in a sigh. "I know."

Lia bent over and plucked one of the items from the pile. A little doll. "So, let's get rid of this doll."

Garr shot to his feet, obviously forgetting for a moment that his foot was bruised and he needed crutches to take the pressure off. She heard Allegra gasp as Tyler rushed past her to grab hold of Garrison's arm. "Whoa, man! What are you doing?"

"I'm *not* getting rid of that," he pointed at the doll she held in her hand. "And it's *not* a doll."

Oooh, he was speaking through clenched teeth. She looked at the thing her fingers were gripping. "Um, yes, it is. It's a boy doll, but a doll nonetheless."

"Take it back."

"Take what back?"

"What you just said. It's not a doll." He faced Tyler, who was still steadying him. "Tell her."

Tyler peered at the doll, then his eyes widened. "Lia. That is totally not a doll."

She dropped her gaze. It was a twelve-inch, hard plastic man with a sleeveless green shirt, camouflage pants, and black boots. "Sure it is. A 'Yo Joe' doll."

"It isn't 'Yo Joe,'" Garrison muttered. "It's *G.I.* Joe."

Lia shrugged. "It's still a doll."

"No." Both men spoke in unison.

This was ridiculous. "Allie, help me out here."

Allegra gingerly stepped over a box and approached Lia, her gaze on the doll. "Hm. Looks like a doll to me."

Tyler rolled his eyes. "Girls. What do they know?"

"'They' know that twelve-inch plastic play things are called dolls." Lia smirked. "This," she held the toy out facing them, "is a doll."

Garrison pointed at it. "That," his voice was low, comically intimidating, "is. Not. A. Doll."

"If it isn't a doll," she asked, "then what is it?"

Both men answered in unison. "An action figure!"

Chapter Eleven

By evening, the "to keep" pile had shrunk and the "giveaway" pile had grown to substantial proportions. If he wasn't careful, Lia would get rid of everything he owned. For a woman who proclaimed she wasn't a neat-freak, she sure did seem to relish purging.

Tyler's phone chirped, drawing his attention. He glanced up at Allie. "It's Bo." He grinned. "Better take this." He slid a finger along the bottom of the phone and lifted it to his ear. "Hey man," he said as he stepped down the hall, his voice fading.

"Well," Allegra fixed her hands on her hips and looked around the living room. "I still can't believe we finished those bookcases. And the boxes."

Lia blew hair out of her face. "It seriously feels like we've moved Mount Everest. That was a lot of stuff."

"Not *that* much, thank you." Garr eyed the red-headed beauty. "And I haven't forgiven you for the doll comment."

She actually snorted. "Uh-huh. I still say it's a doll, but—" she held up a hand to ward off his comeback, "if it makes you feel better, I'll forever refer to it as an action figure."

Forever. The thought of that didn't make him break out in sweat this time. In fact, it even made his heart give an extra thump, like it was high-fiving itself. But wow. They'd only known each other for two days. *Two days, Garr. Careful.*

"We should think about dinner." A soft pink climbed her cheeks. "Um...unless you already have plans, that is. Or would rather be alone. Or..." She bit down on her bottom lip and glanced at Allegra. Hoping for a rescue? Forget Allegra. He'd be her knight in shining armor.

Wow. He made himself want to gag. When had he grown so soft? "Dinner sounds good to me. I could really go for some Indian."

"Mm. Give me a good Chicken Korma any time. And always Naan." Lia rubbed her stomach. "Now I'm starving."

The woman just won some serious points. Anyone who loved Indian food rose to the top of his favorite list right away. "Allie?"

"Uh. Sure. But something mild. I think I might be fighting off a virus and don't want to make things worse."

Tyler entered the living room. "Food? Did someone mention dinner?"

Garrison placed their order before opening another box. "One last one before dinner gets here."

"Perfect," Lia sidled up next to him and peered in. "What's in this one."

Good question. He lifted a small box out, unlatched it, and raised the lid. "Oh wow. Baby pictures."

"What?" Lia grabbed the box from his hands and giggled, the sound washing over him. He watched as she sat on the couch and pulled a few photos out of the box. "Ohmygoodness, you were so cute!" She glanced up at him, her eyes sparkling. "What happened?"

"Everyone's a comedian." He laughed as he moved his crutches to sit beside her. He plucked one from her fingers and grinned. "This is me and my two childhood buddies," he pointed first to himself, then to Nathan and Deshawn. "We always loved playing cops and robbers, so my mom made us some police and prisoner costumes."

"I'm guessing from the black and white striped costume that you were always the robber?"

He grinned. "Caught. Again." He glanced back at the picture. "Deshawn always played the detective who solved the crime and Nathan was always the one who arrested me."

"Do you still keep in touch with them?"

The question stabbed his chest. "With Deshawn. He really is a detective now, in Denver."

"That's too funny. And Nathan? Do you know where he is?"

"Yeah. He enlisted in the Army and deployed to Afghanistan." He tried to swallow past the lump in this throat but could only squeeze the next words out. "Never made it home."

"Oh." Lia was quiet a moment. "I'm sorry, Garrison."

He shrugged, dipping his chin to his chest. "It hurts still, but he died doing what he loved. He was part of the military working dog program. His partner, Apache, was injured trying to save Nathan, but he made it and was adopted by an incredible family." He looked back up. "I would have loved to adopt Apache, but I was in Berlin when he was retired and I didn't know about it until I got back to Seattle. But he seems to be in a good home. I just wish I could have had a little part of my friend."

"Do you ever get to see him?"

Garrison shrugged one shoulder. "Nah. The program didn't want to give out personal information, and I don't blame them. They reassured me, but that was all they could do."

Talk about putting her foot where her mouth is. Ugh. But she couldn't have known about Nathan. Time to change the subject. "So, what about you? You mentioned you work in cybersecurity and just came back from overseas. What exactly do you do?"

"Uh...well..." Was he hoping she'd let him off the hook? Nope.

"Spill it. What do you do?"

"Do you know much about IT?"

She couldn't lie. "No, not really. I mean, I know how to use a computer." That got a chuckle out of him. She could listen to that deep laugh all day long.

"You've heard of hackers, right?"

No. Uh-uh. He couldn't be a hacker. She was going to go to prison just by association! Her mother always told her to be careful of the company she kept. People would judge her based on her friends. She would have to use her one free call from jail to ask her mom to watch her hamster for her. Poor Jerry! Poor Mom! She was allergic to his bedding. Maybe she could ask one of her friends instead?

"Lia?"

She couldn't go to prison. She had so much to look forward to in life. She didn't want to spend one hour a day outside, lifting weights, getting prison tattoos, and earning the nickname 'Red.' She hated that nickname.

"Lia."

Then again, she wouldn't have to worry about paying her rent. Right? There was always a silver lining. Even to prison. Right? *Right*?

"Lia!"

She jumped in her seat when Garr's hand waved in front of her face. "What?"

"Are you okay? Are you having some kind of seizure?"

"What?"

"You paled and went really still. And you wouldn't respond. Deshawn's sister would get that way when she was having a seizure. It was scary."

He cared. Sweet. "Oh, no. I'm sorry. I'm fine. I was just thinking. You're, um," she swallowed past the huge lump in her throat. "You're a hacker?"

Garrison leaned back into the couch and wiped his forehead with his arm. "You had me worried." He turned his head, resting it against the couch, and smiled. "The hacker you're thinking of is a black hat. Someone who does it illegally. I'm a white hat. An ethical hacker."

"Isn't that kind of an oxymoron?"

There was that rich laugh again. She swore her spine turned to jelly because she wanted to crumple against him and snuggle. She had to nip that feeling in the bud.

"So, what do ethical hackers do?"

He turned his gaze toward the bookcase across the room. "Well, we—" The buzzer sounded on his phone. "Dinner's here!" He let the delivery person in, pushed against the couch to stand, grabbed his crutches, and made his way to the door.

Her mouth watered just thinking about the Chicken Korma to come. And the Naan. Oh, how she loved Naan.

Chapter

Twelve

A white hat?"

Garrison glanced up at Lia then back down to pull the food out of the bag. "Yeah. I basically find weak spots and back doors in programs and networks and hack my way into them so I can then help the others on my team reinforce those to keep the unethical—" he grinned at her— "hackers out."

She nodded. "Sounds interesting."

"It's fun, to be honest. I get to do something malicious but with permission." He winked—winked!—at her, surprising both himself and Lia, if her tucked in lips were any indication.

"So that's what you did in Berlin, too?"

"Yep."

Tyler leaned across the counter and slid the curry onto the ledge. "Our man here also was a board game champion in Berlin."

Lia's brows furrowed at Tyler before she turned back to Garrison. "Board game champion?"

He nodded, pride puffing his chest out. "Ticket to Ride champion, to be exact."

"Oh, do tell." She bent down, resting her elbows on the counter, and batted her eyes at him.

Did his stomach grow butterflies? Because something flew around in there when he looked at her. "Each year, Berlin hosts Gamefest at Säälchen, a cool little space. A friend, Shawn, and I signed up for the tournament just for the fun of it. Turns out, I'm pretty good at Ticket to Ride." He grabbed a crutch, hobbled to a box they hadn't fully unpacked yet, and pulled out a small trophy. He brought it to Lia, showing her the engraved label: *Gamefest Champion: Zug um Zug.*

"Nicely done," she said. No doubt highly impressed. He grinned.

"Hey babe," Tyler called, "come get your dinner."

Garr looked up in time to see Allegra lift the cover off the container, take a whiff, and turn green. The next thing he knew, she was running in the direction of the bathroom. He looked over at his friend who stood there, staring at where Allie had been. "Is she okay?"

"I guess I should go check." Retching drifted down the hall from the bathroom, making it Tyler's turn to go green. His head bobbed and he turned on his heel and raced down the hall.

Lia leaned over the counter and pointed to one of the closed containers. "Is that mine?"

"Yep," he handed her the Korma. "It smells so good."

"Believe me," she dipped her fork in the creamy sauce and licked it, "it sooo is."

Tyler reappeared with his arm wrapped around Allegra. "Hey guys, I think we're going to get out of here."

Garr's heart jumped. The prospect of some time alone to get to know the woman across from him better had him smothering a grin. "Yeah," he kept his voice sober, "totally understandable. Get some rest. I hope you feel better soon, Allie."

"She just needs n—. Ow!" Tyler rubbed his free hand on his side where Allie's arm rested. "Why did you—"

"Thanks Garrison." Allegra moved her gaze to Lia. "It's been so fun getting to know you. We need to hang out more. Oh, and I should introduce you to my friend, Story. You two would love each other."

"That would be great. Thanks."

Garr bagged Tyler and Allegra's food back up and passed it off to his friend. Tyler did a two-finger salute and pulled Allegra out the door. When it clicked shut, Garrison faced Lia. "So. *Goonies?*"

"*Goonies.*" Ugh. "Sure." She could do this. She could watch a kid's movie about a treasure hunt. Right? She peeked at Garrison in the kitchen pouring them some water, a dark lock of hair falling over his forehead and into his eyes. Yeah. She could do this.

Twenty minutes later, she wasn't as sure. She rolled her eyes at the overly dramatic portrayal of the villains. Garr must have caught her—a jab into her arm jolted her gaze from the movie. "What?"

"You're inwardly mocking it, aren't you?"

Busted. "Me?" She laid a hand on her chest, going for an innocent look. She didn't think he was buying it.

She watched as he grabbed the remote and pressed Pause. Nope. He wasn't buying. He turned, the most serious look on his face. Uh-oh. Had she offended him? Disappointed him? The thought caused a wave in her stomach.

"Lia." Garr grabbed her hands. "I don't think I can do this."

That wave turned into a tsunami. "You can't work with me? Pay me?" *Date me?*

"I can't watch *Goonies* with you." His eyes twinkled. "You aren't taking this seriously. There is so much to learn from this movie. What if, one day, you find yourself trapped in a cave with pirates? What will you do?"

She snorted. And the next minute, they both leaned back on the couch, panting from the exertion. Garr turned his head, resting against the back of the couch, and grinned. "I haven't laughed that much in ages."

She shook her head. "You and me both." Lia flicked a glance at the watch on her left wrist. 9:15 PM. "I should go. We'll never finish the movie at this rate anyway."

"Never say never," he winked. He stretched his arms over his head, lifting the T-shirt he wore enough to give a peek at a sliver of flat abdomen. Lia lifted her gaze. No need to ogle the boss. "I don't know if I'll be here in the morning when you arrive. I have to go check on something for work. I could be gone all day, so just go ahead and do what you think is best."

"Why don't I make a pile of things I think you should go through to either donate or throw out? If I run across any photos or board games, I at least have cabinets to put them for now. Once I've unpacked everything, we can go through and truly organize.

He stood and reached his hands out to pull her off the couch. "Sounds like a plan."

"Thanks for dinner, Garrison. I even had fun...until you hit PLAY." She smirked.

Garr grabbed at his chest, a pained look crossing his face. "That wounds, Lia. Wounds."

She walked out the door, laughing. When the elevator dinged and the doors slid open, she glanced over her shoulder. There stood Garrison, hand lifted, a soft smile playing his lips.

It had been more than a fun night. It had been the best night she'd had in as long as she could remember.

She was in trouble.

Chapter

Thirteen

The lock clicked and Lia swung her door open. It had been a long but great day. She always felt good when she was able to accomplish a lot and getting rid of all those boxes in Garrison's place was a *lot*. She dropped her bag on the tiny wood-grain kitchen counter and eyed the orange-wood cabinets. The 1970s vibe had to go, but maybe once the Chancellor was feeling better and she started at Rainier University, her salary would afford her an upgrade in apartment living.

A quiet scratch from the coffin-sized living room caught her attention. "Jerry," she moved to open the cage and lifted the blond hamster out, bringing him to her face. "How was your day?"

Not that she expected him to answer. That would just be crazy. But it was good to be able to come home and talk to someone other than herself, and since her apartment didn't allow cats or dogs, Jerry was the next best thing.

She bent down and opened the door to the dark brown MDF end table. Inside was Jerry's clear exercise ball. She set him down inside the bottom half and attached the top half, then set it on the floor. Jerry took off and started rolling around the apartment.

Lia flopped on the couch, stretching her legs and thought back on the day. Tyler and Allegra were a blast, but the most fun she'd had was with Garrison over the past couple of days. She could still taste the meatball he'd dared her to stuff in her mouth.

Dare...hm. What would be fun to dare him with? She had to keep in mind his injured foot, but surely there was something she could challenge him with. Maybe?

This was going to require a lot of thought. And thought always required hummus and pita chips. She hopped off her couch, barely avoiding Jerry who was running the ball toward the sliding door that led to the balcony. The balcony that was barely big enough for one. And overlooked the alley with the dumpster.

She was living the life.

Lia opened the cupboard and grabbed the lightly salted pita chips, then found the hummus on the lowest shelf of the fridge. She dropped everything on the end table and went back for a drink. Popping the tab on the top of the can, the hiss from carbonation reminded her of Marvin, her old employer's, poor tie. Note, *not* poor Marvin, but his poor *tie*. It probably cost Marvin's wife a good twenty-dollar bill for that tie, and it went up in flames. She still couldn't believe she'd set fire to his tie. Thank goodness for the Coke. Well, she was pretty sure Marvin wasn't thankful for it. But in her panic at setting her boss on fire when she turned in her letter of resignation, she'd found the can, shaken it, and sprayed it all over him. At least it put out the fire. While she may have set fire to him in the first place, he could have at least been happy with her heroic efforts to save him. Alas.

She could still smell the smoking polyester.

Smoke. Huh. That gave her an idea. She scooted forward and picked up her phone from the old glass and brass coffee table. She couldn't wait to update not just her apartment, but the décor, too.

As she tapped a name in her contacts list, she giggled. He wanted to dare and double-dog dare her? Two could play this game.

Morning came far too soon. Lia stretched her arms above her head, knocking her knuckles on the headboard. Thinking back to the prior night's call, she was happy Garrison wouldn't be there today. Between needing to get rid of the toss piles before he changed his mind and hopefully arranging this dare for him, she was going to keep busy.

And she couldn't stop grinning. It was apparent Garrison liked to have fun, and she was happy to oblige.

She readied herself for the day, donning her favorite yoga pants and sweatshirt and threw her hair in a messy bun, fed Jerry, and headed for Garrison's.

❧⊷∞⊶❧

The vibration in his pocket jerked him back to reality. Garr shoved his hand inside and grabbed the phone, not bothering to look at the caller on the screen before he swiped his thumb across the bottom to answer it.

"Hello?"

"Garrison McGarville, please?" The low voice grated across the line.

"Speaking."

"Mr. McGarville, my name is Don Brody. I received your name and number from a mutual friend."

"Don Brody?" The race car driver? Who was their mutual friend? Because he was pretty sure he would have known if he'd had a friend who was friends with this guy. Maybe Tyler. He was into the extreme stuff, and racing was pretty extreme.

"Yessir. I've been asked to pick you up and take you for a spin."

Uh... "A spin? What kind of spin?"

A muffled giggle sounded over the line. And a giggle would only come from a woman, and Tyler wasn't a woman.

He didn't know any women in Seattle yet, with the exception of Allegra and...Lia? What was going on?

"Oh, you know. The usual. Our friend thought you might like to see the car I drive."

He would? He could fully admit to being a geek, however, cars weren't his thing. But the chance to meet one of Seattle's best-known race car drivers? It may not be a normal interest, but... He grinned. Tyler would probably be jealous.

Garr cleared his throat. "Sure? What time and where should I go to meet you?"

"How about right now, downstairs in front of your building?"

Wait...*now*? In the middle of the work day? In front of his office building? "Uh."

More muffled talking from the other end of the line. "Sorry, but this is really the only time I have, and our friend was insistent. They thought you'd love this."

Garrison looked around the office. Most of his colleagues were out on calls or buried deep in front of their computers. A glance at the clock on his own computer screen showed it was almost lunch time. "Sure. Be right down."

"See you in a sec."

He tapped the screen to end the call and sat another moment, staring into space. It was a good thing he was a detective...of sorts. Okay, he was an Internet Security Officer. But still. He had to look for and find the back doors that others with less stellar intentions would find so they could be addressed. And sometimes, he got to look for—and find—those who already found those back doors or otherwise hacked into systems. He'd find out who set this up. If that giggle was any indication, he already had a good idea.

Garr slid his keys off the desk and into his pocket then hustled downstairs—still no elevator for him.

Outside, the bright sun forced him to squint. His gaze immediately hit the car and Don Brody. It was hard to miss the bright blue Porsche 911 GT2 RS. He may not be a car guy, but wow. That was one incredible car. But as hard as it was to miss the beautiful machine, it was the auburn-haired beauty grinning from ear-to-ear standing in front of the car that really caught his attention.

"Lia." Mystery solved even faster than he'd expected.

That grin split even wider. "Surprise!"

"But..." The spark in her eyes lit a fire in his belly. "What's going on?"

"You know how you dared me to stuff an entire meatball in my mouth the other day?"

"Yeeaaaah," he dragged the word out.

"I'm daring you now."

He must have looked as confused as he felt because she just laughed then opened the passenger door. "Your ride awaits."

"I'm seriously getting in there," he pointed his index finger at the black and gray interior, "with a race car driver? Are you insane?"

"C'mon." She then had the audacity to wink at him. "I dare you."

There was a scene in the movie, *Back to the Future*, where Marty McFly was called chicken and it triggered something in the character. Being dared did that to Garrison. He couldn't—and wouldn't—back down from a dare. And it looked like Lia may have caught on to that. Shoot.

He glared at her but couldn't keep a straight face. "Fine," he laughed and crawled into the space. And wow, was it comfortable. More comfortable than he would have thought. In the sideview mirror, he saw Lia lean forward and say something to Don. Why did his stomach suddenly drop?

He didn't have time to think about it—Don slid into the driver's seat. "Buckle up. Let's go for a ride."

Who knew a car could go from zero to breakneck speeds in no seconds flat? He should have expected it but sweat broke out on his upper lip anyway.

"I hope you have some time this afternoon. We're gonna be a while."

"We are?" Was that his voice that ended on a high pitch? He turned his head to make sure Lia hadn't sneaked into the back of the car. Not that there was any room back there.

They made their way out of Seattle, the traffic holding Don's speed back. Soon enough, the high-rises melted into the background and they sped past cars and concrete walls then greenery alongside the Interstate. Don sped up, weaving in between the cars as they raced south.

Garr felt himself pushed back in his seat—or was that his leg pretending to brake that was pushing him back? "You're, uh, going a little fast, aren't you? You don't want to get a ticket."

Don just laughed. "She said you might be nervous. She didn't know if this was your thing." Don's phone rang through the Bluetooth. The driver scrambled to answer the call, turning the Bluetooth off. "Hey." He whispered into the phone, making it hard for Garr to hear what he was saying.

Soon he ended the call. "Our exit is up ahead."

Sure enough, he pulled off and headed east. The trees rose up on each side, showing off their spring green. He normally preferred fall and winter, but days like this when the sun was out and the skies were clear, the green was spectacular. There was a reason they called Seattle and area the Emerald City.

A short while and another exit later, they turned down a few more streets and pulled up to a race track.

Garr's stomach fell. He'd withstood the beading sweat on his upper lip as Don drove. He'd even withstood his own white knuckles. But a raceway? Uh...

He swallowed. Hopefully Don didn't hear the gulp. "What are we doing here?"

Don flashed perfectly white, straight teeth his direction. "I'll let her tell you." He tilted his chin up, looking out the passenger seat's window. Garr turned his head, his gaze connecting with Lia.

Lia? How did she beat them here?

She opened his door and bowed, sweeping her hand toward the entrance. "Your carriage awaits."

Bees were stinging inside his belly. No way. No how. One big emphatic 'no.' "My carriage? The only carriage I'm getting into is one drawn by a horse."

The woman had the gall to laugh. She laughed! "Come on." Lia held out her hand.

He was never one to refuse the soft hand of an auburn beauty.

Come to think of it, he'd never been offered the soft hand of an auburn beauty before. He was a geek in the truest sense: more into his computers, board games, and movies than he was into dating. But there was something about this woman that drew him. And for some reason, she seemed drawn to him, too.

He took her hand. Warmth radiated from her...or was that warmth from him? He was sure he felt a slow burn tingling through his body.

Lia's brown-sugar gaze startled. She bit down on her bottom lip before looking over his shoulder. "Don."

He'd never known disappointment to be so bitter. Did those two have a thing? He dropped her hand before turning to face the taller man.

Don stepped up next to Lia and wrapped an arm around her. Garrison's stomach churned. Who was he kidding? A woman like her would never go for a guy like him. He may not be necessarily ugly, but he had way different interests than other men his age. She was out of his league.

Wasn't she?

Don leaned down, his longer blond hair falling into his eyes. "How did you get here so fast?"

"I learned to drive from the best," she grinned.

"That's what cousins are for."

His heart flipped. Cousins? They were cousins? Why didn't she mention that? He could have avoided at least two minutes of emotional roller coaster. Maybe Tyler was right and he needed to ask her out. If he was feeling this jealous over a *cousin*...

"So, Garrison. Are you ready?"

His scalp prickled. "Ready for what?"

Lia's eyes sprinkled mischief all over the place. "To hop in a race car with the best," she elbowed Don's stomach. Her *cousin's* stomach. Man, that felt good to know.

Wait. What? "Hop in a race car? Isn't that what I drove here in?" He swallowed. "Nah, I'm good. You two go ahead."

"I've been."

She was a little daredevil, wasn't she? She'd have fun hanging out with Tyler and his crew. "You have?"

"You can't grow up with Don Brody as your cousin and not be at the race track on a regular basis. So, it's your turn. Two hundred miles per hour."

He sputtered. The woman was off her rocker.

"No way."

The look on her face—the little smile playing her lush lips, the eyebrows rising, the little dimple forming on one cheek—should have been his clue to get out of Dodge. But did he? No.

He shook his head once. And again. "No, for real. I'm good."

"I double-dog dare you."

Chapter

Fourteen

She knew she had him when his cheeks flushed and his eyes narrowed. Thankfully, she'd pegged him right. He couldn't turn down a dare.

Lia wanted so badly to laugh, but she was afraid she'd break the spell if she did. Instead, she waited, as patient as a spider waiting in its web for dinner. She rubbed her hands together. Okay, maybe not so patient.

Garrison's head started swinging from side-to-side. "Shouldn't you be organizing something right now?"

Yep, she had him. "I worked this morning, and thanks to your credit card," she waggled her eyebrows, "I'm waiting for some floating shelves to show up."

His mouth worked but no sound came out. Uh-oh. She'd placed the order without asking him. Was he angry? There was one way she could make this better. "The shelves are to display your Star Wars LEGO creations."

That did it. His eyes grew as wide as his smile. "Sweet!"

Bullet dodged. She didn't know if he would have truly been angry with her—he'd mentioned in passing the night they'd tried to watch the kid's movie that she could get what she needed with his card—but it was still a risk since she didn't know him all that well.

She hoped that would change.

Heat crawled up her neck. She wasn't going to think about it right now. She had a dare to enforce.

"So?" Lia waved her hand over her shoulder. "Do I need to triple-dog dare you?"

He growled. "Woman, you are going to be the gorgeous bane of my existence!"

Gorgeous? The heat moved from her neck to her cheeks. Ooohh...she was going to tuck that one away to savor later.

He continued, eyeing Don. "Am I going to die?"

Her cousin's laugh echoed as they headed for the track. "I haven't killed anyone yet."

"Not so reassuring, thanks," Garr mumbled.

It was a quiet day on the track, thanks to the mid-week work crowd. Don readied the car, a black Camaro ZL1. "Whoa, Cuz. This is a new one." Lia ran a hand over the glossy metal.

"Yeah," Don grinned. "It's the model we'll be racing this upcoming season. I thought Garrison here would like a spin."

"No, no. I wouldn't want you to get in trouble for taking me out. I'm good."

Lia slid a hand over her mouth. No way would she want Garrison seeing her laugh.

"It's all good man," Don slapped Garr's shoulder. She wasn't sure if Garrison's wince was in fun or real, but she had a suspicion it was real. Don didn't know his own strength half the time.

"Uh..."

Lia peered closely at Garrison's hands. They were shaking. Was he nervous? "Remember," she said. "I double-dog dared you."

Oh, if looks could kill, she'd be lying flat on the ground. Too bad. She wasn't going to let him out of this one.

Lia filled her lungs. "You ready?"

Her cousin grinned. "Always."

"Garrison?" He traveled the world, was friends with an extreme sports enthusiast. It was almost unbelievable to think he'd be nervous about this.

Then again, traveling at 200 miles per hour made most sane people nervous.

"Let's motor." Don snickered before he strode to the gleaming car waiting for him. Lia watched as he slid his helmet on, then lifted one leg through the driver's side window, straddled the frame, and lifted the other leg in, sliding down into the seat.

She glanced at Garr's profile and almost laughed out loud. He stood there, slack-jawed, before he pointed. "Am I supposed to do that?"

"How else are you going to get in?"

He eyed her. "Open the door?"

Honest, she couldn't stop the smirk, even if she wanted to. And she didn't. "With what door handle?"

His squinted gaze flew to the car. He straightened, turned, and grabbed her by the shoulders. "How do I get out if there's an accident? A fire? Am I going to die?"

He was bordering on hysteria. And she was about to lose it. Her stomach hurt from clenching back the laughter. "No, you won't die. You'll climb back out. And there won't be an accident or a fire. There aren't any other cars on the track, and Don has been doing this as long as I can remember. You'll be fine." She moved behind him and shoved him toward the car. "Now go!"

If ever there was a man who looked like he was walking to his death, it was Garrison McGarville.

~⚬~

The smell of burning rubber filled his nostrils. But more than that, it was the fear that filled his soul. He was sure he wouldn't die...but no one said anything about not being maimed.

"Is this really safe?" he shouted over the engine revving.

No answer. Hm. Should he take that as Don just didn't hear him, or more like he just hit the nail on the head and this wasn't safe?

Gravity pushed him back in his seat—the one that took him five minutes of fumbling and pain to get into. He'd seen Lia holding her stomach, a sure sign she was laughing harder than she ought to. But then, it was kinda fun to be the guy to put a smile on her face.

And she was so going to pay.

Don had them whipping around the curves, speeding so fast he couldn't see the trees, walls, Lia, nothing. All he could see was the dark grey pavement in front of them and Don beside him. But he did notice one thing: the sweat that had broken out when he first learned what was about to happen was now cold, like an ice cube gliding down his back.

Maybe he *was* going to die. He could relate so much better to Allegra now when she'd once told him about Tyler taking her hang gliding. He'd never thought of himself as a 'scaredy cat,' but he wasn't ashamed to admit that he wasn't one for doing extreme things. And he would qualify race car driving—er, riding—as extreme.

Six laps into it—which didn't equate to much time considering the high speeds—he noticed that he wasn't as tense. Gravity still held him in but he felt his lips curve up. Was he actually having fun? Say it wasn't so! But he was. And he had Lia to thank for this.

And thank her he would.

Chapter

Fifteen

She dearly hoped he was a forgiving soul. After watching him struggle to get his long frame into the car—including his helmet-encased head he'd hit on the frame more than once—and watching them whip around the track, she was pretty sure he would never ask her out. More likely, he'd fire her on the spot. Lia swallowed the growing lump in her throat.

This was a bad, bad idea. What made her think she could dare a man—her *boss*—she'd only known a few days? What made her think she knew him that well after he dared her to eat a meatball? A meatball! It wasn't like it was anything she didn't like to start with. Who wouldn't like the Swedish meatballs from that store? And they weren't even all that big to stuff an entire one in her mouth. Seriously. She was out of her mind. To go from a meatball-eating dare to a "jump in a race car and go over 200 miles per hour" dare.

Yep. She was so fired.

The roar of the engine preceded the car. She watched as Don slowed the Camaro down to a stop in front of her. At least he hadn't slammed the brakes as he liked to do when he had a newbie in the car with him. Maybe Garrison was screaming for mercy in there and Don obliged him.

Yeah, no. That didn't sound like Don. Was something wrong?

Her cousin pulled himself out of the vehicle and scurried to Garr's side, drawing his helmet off as he moved on fast feet. He looked over his shoulder at Lia. "Help me pull him out?"

She rushed forward and grabbed Garrison under one arm as Don talked him through climbing out while he pulled under the other arm.

When Garrison was fully out, he bent over, hands resting on his knees.

"Do you want me to get your helmet off for you?"

He shook his head but didn't say anything.

They stood in silence another moment before Garrison straightened and lifted the helmet off his head. Under that protection, his hair stuck to his head as sweat rolled down his green face.

Oh. No.

She was definitely fired.

"Are you okay?"

He squeezed his eyes shut before they sprung open, staring right at her. "I didn't know I get car sick."

Don chuckled—not helping! "Were you focused on the track or on the surroundings?"

Garrison glared at him. "How could I focus on anything going that fast?"

Her cousin nodded. "So, you were trying to focus."

Her soon-to-be-former boss just stared.

"Yep. You were. That's why you got sick. Racing that fast while trying to keep an eye on your surroundings rather than just the pavement in front of you will get you in trouble."

"Obviously." The flat timbre of Garrison's voice formed ice in the pit of her stomach. She'd blown it. Maybe she should sneak off to her car right now, before he could catch her. Don would drive him back, and that would give Garr time to cool down. And forgive her.

Too late. The man of the hour did an about-face, catching her. "Not so fast."

"Remember, Garrison. 'Forgive one another, as God in Christ forgave you.'"

He nodded in slow motion. "Ephesians."

She felt her eyebrows jump up.

"You forgot the first half of that verse. 'Be kind to one another, tenderhearted.' This wasn't so kind. Or tenderhearted, Lia Walker."

The louse she called family spoke up. "I'm out." He pointed at Lia. "You can drive him back to Seattle." The coward walked off and actually left her alone with an angry man. He was so not getting a Christmas gift this year. She gathered the courage to look Garrison in the eyes.

Was he really angry? There was something in his look that told her she might be in trouble, but not the way she was thinking. She tried to examine it, but it was gone before she had more time. Instead he jutted his chin toward the exit. "Let's go."

Lia trailed after him, reluctant to spend an hour plus in the car alone with him. It would be awkward, especially once he fired her.

Too soon, she sat behind the wheel of her clunker car and turned the key in the ignition. The engine purred to life and they left the race track behind.

The first half hour was quiet. Quieter than she was comfortable with, at least right now. She glanced over at Garrison several times, but he was on his phone or looking out the window.

She cleared her throat. "So..." She looked over in time to see him side-eye her.

"So."

Yeah, this wasn't going well. She just prayed traffic was good going back into the city so they didn't have to prolong this awkward car ride.

Another seven minutes of silence—not that she was counting—as the trees whizzed past their windows. Finally,

finally Garrison coughed. Did that mean he was about to say something? Anything? She'd even take the answered suspense of whether she was fired or not right now.

She couldn't wait to get home and snuggle with Jerry, if her on-the-go hamster would let her.

He probably wouldn't, the little traitor.

She waited, but even after the cough, Garrison didn't say anything. She was doomed.

"I'm not going to fire you."

She was so desperate to hear from him, she imagined him telling her she wasn't fired.

"Promise."

She was really losing it. Making up a conversation in her own mind probably bordered on needing a doctor's appointment. Or becoming a writer. Didn't writers make up full-on conversations in their heads? She'd save money—maybe even make money—if she turned to writing rather than seeing a psychologist. She would have to Google 'how to be a writer' when she got home. But what genre would she write in? Maybe "what not to do." Was that a genre? She could make it one and be a pioneer of the publishing industry. That would be kind of cool.

"Lia?" A hand waved in front of her face.

Waving his hand in her vision probably wasn't the best idea, if the slamming on her brakes was any indication. He was grateful there wasn't any traffic right behind them, but he might need to get checked for whiplash by a doc.

"I'm sorry. I didn't mean to scare you."

Lia checked the rearview mirror and floored the gas pedal. It was like being back in the race car again.

His stomach churned. Not a great memory, even if he had to admit it was kind of fun.

"Did you hear what I said, though? About not firing you?"

He confessed he'd thought about it for a nanosecond, but she'd been doing a great job buying furniture for his place and unpacking and organizing his things...and his apartment was still a mess. When he looked up from making reservations on his phone and saw her pale cheeks, he'd guessed at what she was thinking. Was he right?

"Thank you." He almost didn't hear her whispered words. He had to put this woman out of her misery. At least he thought she was in misery.

"No, I have to thank you." She glanced his way. "Never in a million years would getting in a race car have crossed my mind." He grinned. "I mean, don't get me wrong. I've played *Formula D* but wouldn't have ever thought of actually being in one."

"What's *Formula D?*"

First *Goonies* then his G.I. Joe action figure, now *Formula D?* She wounded him. "It's an auto race board game."

"Huh."

And that's all she had to say about that. Sad.

"We'll play it some time."

"We will?"

He folded his arms across his chest and turned in his seat to face her. "We will."

A smile eased onto her face. That was more like it.

"Have dinner with me?"

The smile dropped a moment before his stomach did. Oh no. Did he just blow it?

"To go over plans to organize the rest of your home?"

Is that what she wanted? Or was she hoping it was more than that? He hated dating, not that he did much of it. But trying to figure someone out when he didn't really know them wasn't his forte.

"It's just dinner." Was that vague enough? He watched her mouth...to see if she gave any clues as to what she was thinking, of course. Not because he was thinking about those lips. No.

Speaking of those lips, they pursed. "Just dinner?"

Yeah, he hated dating. What was she thinking? He could just come out and ask her straight up. She might be the kind who liked being upfront about things so she didn't have to guess. Him? Deep fry him because he was a chicken.

Chapter

Sixteen

What, exactly, was he asking her? On a date? Or was this a working dinner? Ugh. She didn't like not knowing what he was getting at. This was one of the many reasons she didn't date often. Well, that and no one asked her.

Hmph. Men.

With her hands at the ten-and-two position on her steering wheel, she glanced at Garrison. He sat there, watching her. Uh...why? What was he looking at? Did she have something on her face? Grease from the track?

"I'm debating something."

He read her like a book. She couldn't decide if this was a good thing or not.

Her car hit a bump on the highway, forcing her to look forward again. It was a welcome distraction. Not that driving should be the distraction.

"What are you debating?"

"Whether I should explain or not." He mumbled something then blew out a harsh breath.

Up ahead was an exit that led to a coffee house. Maybe they could go there and sit down to hash whatever was bugging him out. Was he thinking of firing her, despite what he'd said? Maybe that's why he'd asked her to dinner. To let her down gently, over a good meal. But he'd mentioned playing a board game. Maybe he wanted to fire her but remain friends.

That was a lot of "maybe's."

She turned on her signal to exit.

"Where are we going?"

"I think we need to talk, so let's hit up a coffee shop."

He was silent a moment before, "That sounds like a good idea."

They pulled into the parking lot. Garrison held the door open for her and even paid for her coffee, despite finding coffee drinkers suspicious people. She swallowed. Was this really the end? Or did he have something else in mind?

When they sat at a small table across from one another, Garrison twisted the cup of tea in his hands. Lia turned the lid on the disposable cup so the opening wasn't sitting on the seam, then sipped her latte, leaving Garrison to start the conversation when he was ready.

It took a bit, but he finally looked up and opened his mouth. "I don't know how to start. I'm not used to this...especially when it's important to me."

"Important to you?"

"Yeah." He looked down at his cup. "I've had a great time since we met."

"Me too."

Garrison looked back up, a smile playing on his lips. "I'm glad. And you're doing great work at my place."

Lia smiled. "I feel like I've hardly been there to even do much of anything. You're paying me to organize your home, and I've been dragging you from work to the race track."

"Only today. Besides," he grinned. "You *did* double-dog dare me."

"I have plans for tomorrow." She squelched the laughter at his widened gaze. "Those shelves I ordered should be delivered."

He leaned back and swiped his arm across his forehead. "You had me worried there for a minute. I thought maybe another dare was coming."

"I'm not that mean." She grinned. "I figured you could use a day off. Besides, I also plan on getting your bedroom closet in order tomorrow. Those games took care of a lot of boxes, though."

"I do have room to walk now."

"I can't believe how many board games you own."

He just shrugged. "What can I say? I'm a connoisseur."

"Oh, you're something." She grabbed a napkin from the roughened wood table and started tearing up the edges. "So...what was it you were thinking of explaining?"

Garrison shifted in his seat then folded his hands in front of him on the table. This couldn't be a good sign.

When did she become such a pessimist?

"I meant what I said, I'm not firing you, Lia."

She sat back in her chair, a rush of air huffing from her mouth. "Thank you."

"I figured that would give you a bit of relief."

She pointed at him. "You figured right." She leaned forward, resting her elbows on the table and her face in her hands. "So?"

He watched her for a moment, his dark gaze roving over her face. He almost seemed hesitant.

"Well, I—"

Raised voices at the front of the store interrupted whatever Garr was about to say. They both looked in that direction to see a blond woman standing over a man dripping in iced coffee. Oooh, that had to be cold. Lia could see a couple of ice cubes sitting on the collar of his shirt before the man swiped them off.

"You jerk!" The woman had no qualms at all expressing her feelings for the man.

"I can't help being deployed." He didn't shout, but he wasn't quiet.

"You promised you wouldn't go out for at least another year."

Garrison had fully turned around by this time, watching the spectacle, but looked over his shoulder at her, eyes wide. She shrugged.

"Joslyn, you know my life isn't my own. I go and do whatever the government tells me to. It wasn't my choice to deploy again."

Lia wiped a hand across her eyes. She felt for this Joslyn woman, but the guy was right. She'd had a couple of friends in the military, and for the most part, they weren't offered the choice.

"I can't do this again. If you're going to go back over to that sandbox, or whatever you people call it, I'm out of here."

Another customer shouted from behind Lia, "Good riddance!" She slid down in her seat when the couple looked over, Joslyn's face red with anger, and the guy's face pink, no doubt from embarrassment.

Joslyn slip her purse strap on her shoulder. "Goodbye, Jeremy. Enjoy playing war."

Lia's mouth gaped. Did that woman just tell someone to *enjoy playing war*?

Garrison pushed his chair back from the table, went to the counter and whispered to the barista. A minute later, he had an iced coffee in hand and was sitting across from Jeremy. She couldn't hear what they were saying, but warmth flooded her as she watched Garrison lean forward, clap Jeremy's shoulder, then bow his head. Jeremy sat there for a second watching the top of Garrison's head, then bowed his own head. Tears pricked her eyes at the sight of the two men praying.

Garr was definitely a special man.

When they were done, Garrison left Jeremy sitting there and made his way back to Lia. She looked around his tall form to see another person sit down with the service member. It looked like he was going to be okay, especially if he hung out in this coffee shop a few more minutes. She watched Garr as he sat across from her. "You're an incredible guy, you know that?"

His cheeks flushed. "Nah, I'm not. No one needs a public dressing down. Especially when whatever is going on isn't their fault. It's not like he can help being sent off."

She shook her head. This was a humble man, too. She liked him more and more.

"So," he said, "as I was saying."

She sat up in her chair. This was it. Butterflies flitted in her stomach.

"I do want to take you out for dinner, but not for work." He spoke in a rush, as if he was nervous. "I want to do it because..."

She waited. "Because?"

"Because," he swallowed hard enough to be heard, "because I like you."

She swore her heart skipped a beat. Or three. "You like me?" Did that squeak come from her?

Surely the sound disappearing from the coffee shop and the tunnel vision that ensured all he could hear and see was Lia didn't mean he was dying. But man, oh man. If she didn't respond soon, he was probably going to at least melt under the table. Her last question *'You like me?'* came out as an adorable squeak, but she'd just sat there, staring at him since. Even after he nodded—because the thought of talking at the moment sounded impossible.

His mind scrambled to come up with something to convince her. Then he had it.

"I double-dog dare you."

Yep, that got her attention. "Say what?"

"You heard me. I double-dog dare you."

"To do what?" He smothered a laugh at her incredulous look.

"To go for dinner with me."

"Dinner? You already asked me for dinner, but the other day said it was for business."

That was true, he had, but he wanted more than a business dinner. He wanted a date and thought she might too. Had he read her wrong? He could fully admit that when it came to women, he had no game whatsoever.

He gulped. Now or never. "Yeah. Dinner, but not for business. A date. With me."

"Not for business?"

"Nope."

"Or as a way to gently let me down and fire me?"

This woman was deaf. "I already told you—twice—I'm not firing you."

She grinned. "I just had to be extra sure." Her top teeth pulled her bottom lip in. Oh man.

Garr cleared his throat. "So yeah. A date. What do you say?"

Her brown gaze sparkled. "Well, you *did* double-dog dare me. It's impossible to turn that down."

Yeah. He liked this woman.

Chapter

Seventeen

His breath was ripped from his chest when Lia opened the door. The dark skinny jeans fit her to perfection, and the white sleeveless shirt with the big rose pattern in reds, yellows, blues, and pinks set off her auburn hair.

"Hi." She tilted her head to the side, a tiny smile lighting her face.

"Hi." He swallowed. "You look...beautiful."

Her smile widened. "You do, too." She coughed. "Uh, handsome, though. You look handsome. Not beautiful. Because that'd just be weird."

The color infusing her cheeks was too fun. He whisked his hands out to the side then brought one back into his waist and bowed. "Thank you, my lady."

He stood to see her laughing. Yeah, he was a nerd, but if he put a smile on her face, that's all that mattered to him.

"Let me grab my sweater. Are you sure you won't tell me where we're going?"

"Positive." He stepped through her doorway into the tiny apartment. "This is your place? It's nice."

"Dated. And small."

"That too."

Something hard bounced off his ankle. He looked down to see a clear plastic ball with something fluffy inside. The ball moved, and he jumped back. "What in the world?"

Lia poked her head around the corner and laughed. "Oh, that's Jerry, my hamster."

"You have a hamster? Aren't those pets for little kids?"

She came fully around the corner, hands on her hips. "What are you saying, Mr. McGarville?"

He whipped his gaze to her. "Uh, nothing. I promise. I just..." His voice trailed off when he saw the laughter in her eyes. Eyes he could drown in.

"It's okay," she grinned. "You probably don't hear too often of adults having hamsters for pets, but it gets lonely living by yourself—"

Didn't he know that.

"—and I'm not allowed cats or dogs in this place, so I found Jerry at the pet store one day and rescued him from a terrible fate." She leaned closer, cupped a slim hand around her mouth and whispered. "Being owned by a 4-year-old."

He laughed. "That was very noble of you."

It was her turn to curtsey. "Thank you kindly." She stood. "Where are we going?" She pushed her arms into the sleeves of a yellow sweater, slid her feet into a pair of white flats, and grabbed a white something or other that women stuff things into. What was the word? Purse? No, those had a strap, this was one she just held in her hands.

Gah, what did he know? And who really cared? All he saw was one beautiful woman with a smile to bring him to his knees.

"Garrison?"

"Huh?"

"You were staring." The pink that had earlier colored her cheeks now moved down her throat. His eyes followed its trail before he realized what he was doing. He coughed and met her gaze once more. "Where are we going?"

"To my guilty pleasure."

She stepped back, her hand moving to her chest. What—
"No! No. Nothing like that." If she thought what he thought
she was thinking... "No. My guilty pleasure," he ducked his
head, "is karaoke."

Her hand dropped. "Karaoke? You?"

"Hey, I like to sing."

Lia's brows lifted.

"I do. It's fun. And no one cares what you sound like."
He shrugged. "Most of the time."

"But...karaoke? You don't want me to sing, do you?"

He displayed what he hoped was a devilish grin.

"No. No way, no how. No."

"You have to."

She shook her head. "No, I don't."

"Oh, but you do."

"What makes you say that? Because I don't."

"I double-dog dared you. And you agreed."

Lia narrowed her gaze. "You only double-dog dared me
to go for dinner with you."

"I double-dog dared you to go on a date with me. A date
that includes karaoke."

"Not true. You said dinner."

"I remember it differently."

"You remember wrong." She folded her arms across her
chest.

"It's still part of the dare." He had her and he knew it.

"You're a brat."

He smirked. "I know you are, but what am I?"

Who knew she could punch that hard? Garr clutched his
left arm where she'd hit him and laughed.

"You're an immature brat."

"Guilty as charged."

⋘∞⋙

They sat at a small, wooden table for two. A waitress
came by and took their orders—a bleu cheese burger and iced
tea for Garrison, and a cheesesteak and diet Coke for her.

As the karaoke bar filled up around them, the murmur of voices grew louder, making small talk hard, which didn't help her nerves.

He truly was a good-looking guy. A lock of espresso-brown hair kept falling over his eyes, his high cheekbones framing a strong nose above bow-shaped lips. Kissable bow-shaped lips.

Aaaannnndddd...she was done. There was no way she should be thinking about her boss like that. Then again, he *did* have her out on a date. So maybe it was okay to think that way. Good, even, because if she couldn't think of him in a more 'romantic' way, she shouldn't be on a date with him.

She was *so* glad to be on a date with him.

Their waitress set their orders in front of them, steam rising from her cheesesteak.

"Do you mind if I pray?" Garrison looked over and winked.

Heaven help her.

"Not at all. I'd like that." And she would. It was an honor to be with someone unashamed of his faith.

He finished praying and picked up his burger, bowing his head in the direction of her cheesesteak. "It's good to be on a date with someone who will actually eat instead of munching on rabbit food."

She laughed. "I've never had any issues with eating. It might catch up with me some day—already has if our little chase through your apartment lobby and down the street was any indication—but I'll be happy in the meantime." She took a bite of her sandwich, chewed, and swallowed. "I could never be a model."

Garr held his burger up to her. "Cheers to that."

They made quick work of their food, the music starting just as they finished. First one person, then another, and another got up to sing. Everything from old '50s music to new releases blasted throughout the room. Every once in a while, she could hear Garr singing along, but it was too loud to hear how good—or not—he was.

She leaned over during a loud Pat Benatar song to yell in his ear. "When are you getting up there?"

His eyes sparked when he looked her way. "After you."

"Nuh-uh. Not gonna do it."

"Oh yes you are. But I'll give you a break and let you go on after me."

"How kind," she deadpanned.

Garr hopped up from his chair and strutted to the front. He talked to the host, climbed up on the stage, grabbed a mic and grinned at her.

He was a charming one.

The first chords of piano music started and the crowd cheered. Soon, Garrison's voice belted out. "Just a small-town girl, living in a lonely world." Hollers and cat-calls joined in, but Lia heard his voice. It was amazing. *He* was amazing.

And he'd asked *her* out. To sing karaoke. Oh man, was he ever going to regret it.

He reached the chorus and had the entire room joining in, including her. Garrison strutted across the stage, pointing to people, totally hamming it up. He was in his element, and it made her laugh. She loved this side of him.

All too soon the song ended. He crooked a finger at her, beckoning her up on stage.

No. No, no, no, no, no. Not yet. Please not yet. He didn't know what he was asking her to do. He didn't know what he was about to put everyone through, including him. Garr didn't let up, though, so she stood and put one foot in front of the other, as if walking to her death. She sure felt like she was, or at least the death of her relationship with her employer—potential boyfriend?—before it even started.

She whispered her song choice to the host who nodded, then she turned to get up on stage. Garrison held a hand out to help her up. When she stepped up, he didn't let go of her hand, and instead pulled her close to him until their faces were only inches apart. He didn't say anything, his warm breath fluttering across her face. His lips parted as his gaze moved from hers to her mouth.

Whoa nelly. Fire ignited in her veins. Would he really kiss her up here in front of a crowd?

As if he read her thoughts, he blinked and leaned back, the moment broken. She dropped her gaze to his hand as he held the mic out to her. Yeah. She should take that.

Grasping the mic in her hand, she stepped toward center stage and faced the crowd. Ooohhh, she shouldn't have done that. Her stomach clenched. This wouldn't end well. She'd be heckled and run out of town.

The opening notes of Bon Jovi's *Livin' On a Prayer* started. An appropriate song considering what was about to happen.

"Once upon a time not so long ago..." The song's tune was good and robust. Her voice? She sounded like a dying cow, if the audience's faces were a giveaway.

Lia turned to catch a glimpse of Garrison's face. Oh yeah. The deer-in-headlights look. That was one she was used to seeing when she sang in church. The people next to her would stare at her, mouths gaping. She used to be embarrassed by it, but now she just found it funny. Except for this moment, in front of Garrison. Her face burned, but she kept singing. Or would it be considered caterwauling?

"Woah, we're half way there..."

Definitely caterwauling. She looked out into the audience and saw a couple grimacing. *Believe me, it's as painful for me as it is for you.*

It took some long, excruciating moments, but finally—finally!—the song finished. Lia practically ran off the stage...and straight into Garrison. *Oomph.*

"I'm so sorry!"

"We seem to bump into each other often."

She breathed out a laugh. "At least twice."

"It's kinda nice," he waggled his brows, making her laugh again.

"So, um...please tell me you'll never bring me to karaoke again?"

Garrison's laugh tucked her under a blanket of warmth. "Would you be offended if I promised?"

Hm. Would it be okay to wallop a man in public? Mind you, she'd set fire to one, sooo... She fisted her hand and smacked his bicep.

The most glorious thing happened. Garr leaned forward and kissed the top of her head. How sweet it was.

Chapter
Eighteen

A look around Garrison's apartment told her she was almost finished there. It'd been almost two weeks since they did karaoke together and she hadn't seen him since. Two mornings after karaoke, he'd left a note for her on the dark granite kitchen counter telling her work got busy and he was doing overtime, but she hadn't had any other notes, emails, texts, or calls. Not that she was expecting them.

Okay, she was.

But all that free time without being distracted by her temporary employer had her workload inside his home rapidly disappearing. The shelving had arrived so she could display his geeky things. She'd also been given carte blanche to order any other furniture she thought he might need. Lucky for him, she hadn't gone too crazy, but she had bought him a small, black-painted dining table and chairs, along with a chair and couple of storage ottomans for his living room. She viewed the open living area with a critical eye, happy with the greys, blacks, and whites. All he needed was some wall décor for color and he'd be good. And she'd be done. She tried to ignore the disappointment burrowing in her heart.

Her phone buzzed with a text. Scurrying to her purse on the counter, she rummaged through it to find the mobile. Sliding her thumb along the bottom, she opened the screen and tapped on her messages app.

Garrison: *Hey, I just heard from Grandpa.*

Lia: *Oh! How is he?*

Garrison: *Way better. He's planning on returning to work. I'd told him about hiring you, so he asked me to let you know you can expect to hear from him today.*

Lia looked up. Oh. It really was over. She was excited about working for Chancellor McGarville, but she loved what she'd been doing at Garrison's. Her thumbs flew across the keyboard.

Lia: *I'm so happy for him, and you. And I'm excited to get to work for him. Did he tell you when?*

Garrison: *Yep. Monday.*

Today was Thursday. One more day, which was exactly what she needed to finish here, and she could start her new job. It was what she'd wanted. Right?

Lia: *Thanks, Garr. I'll be done here tomorrow anyway.*

She waited while the three dots on the bottom of the screen moved, indicating he was typing.

Garrison: *You've done an incredible job, Lia. Thank you. I've loved what you've done.*

She smiled at the screen. *Thanks, Garr.*

Garrison: *Maybe you can work on my car next.*

Lia burst into laughter. She'd seen his car and while it wasn't nearly as bad as his home was, it could use a good cleaning. And to think, he'd only been in town just over a month.

As her thumbs hovered over the small keyboard, she thought about how to respond for a moment before the perfect answer came to her.

Lia: *As you wish.*

There were no more texts from Garrison as she tidied up and locked his door behind her. Nothing else the rest of the evening.

And no note or word from him the next day as she hung some of his posters on the walls and did a final clean.

Not one word.

All he could think of was her last text to him. "As you wish." Did she know what that famous movie quote actually meant? Westley always responded to Buttercup's demands with that phrase. Buttercup took forever to understand that Westley's response was his way of telling her he loved her.

Surely Lia wasn't saying she loved him. They'd only known one another a couple of weeks. But maybe...maybe she was saying she liked him? She was interested? He'd been a jerk and not talked to her after their date. Work had become busy with another cyberattack he and his team had been laboring night and day to clear out and fight back. They finally had it under control, but was it too late for Lia? When he hadn't answered her last text, was that it? Did she give up on him?

He'd gotten home late Friday night to find his apartment perfect. At least, perfect for him. Lia had even surprised him by having his *Goonies* 'Never say die' T-shirt framed and hung above his couch.

She was amazing.

He'd had every intention of waking up Saturday morning and calling her to see if she'd meet him for breakfast. Instead, he'd woken up to a phone call from his supervisor asking him to come back into work for another attack.

He was coming to hate computers and the Internet.

Now it was Tuesday, and he finally had a day off to make up for working through the weekend. Lia would have started her new job with his grandfather at Rainier University the day before. He wondered how Grandpa would take to him showing up and taking his secretary out for lunch?

No time like the present to find out.

He dressed carefully in dark jeans, a white V-neck T-shirt, and a navy sport coat. It was more for the Chancellor's sake than Lia's, he told himself.

Yeah, he snorted. *Right.*

With one last look in the mirror, he clambered down the building stairs, found his car, and made his way to the university.

Traffic had him drumming his fingers on the steering wheel, but he finally made it. He walked down the plush burgundy-carpeted halls with rich wood paneling on the walls and paintings of previous chancellors staring down. Were they approving or disapproving? Was he insane for even wondering?

As he turned the corner, Lia came into view, sitting at her desk in an open area, right where she'd run into him when they first met. He stopped to watch her for a moment.

Creepy? Maybe. But he loved watching her. She took his breath away.

He cleared his throat as he moved toward her, hoping he wouldn't scare her. She looked deep in thought. At the sound of his cough, Lia's gaze lifted and met his.

"Garrison!"

The lift of her voice gave him hope. Like she was glad to see him. "Hi."

Man, he was lame. *Hi* was all he could come up with?

Lia stood, showing off her long dark-green dress. The color suited her.

"Are you here to see your grandfather?"

Here went nothing. "No. I was hoping to take you for lunch."

Her mouth formed a silent O.

"Are you free?"

She flicked her eyes to the watch on her slender wrist. "Uh, yeah. Let me check with the Chancellor, though." She turned to walk through the door then hesitated and looked back over her shoulder at him. "Why don't you come in and say hi?"

A text buzzed his phone. He groaned. *Impeccable timing.* He lifted the phone up. "Let me answer this. Go on ahead and maybe just tell him I'll catch him when we get back from lunch?"

Lia nodded then disappeared through the door. He'd just finished answering the message from Tyler when she reappeared.

"All good to go?" He tucked the phone into his pocket.

She nodded. "Where do you want to go? The cafeteria?"

Rainier University might be known for its good food, but a cafeteria wasn't exactly what he had in mind. "Let's go off campus somewhere. You like sushi?"

He watched her face, fascinated. He didn't know it was possible for someone to literally turn as green as her dress.

"Um..."

Time to take pity on her because that was an obvious no. "How about Thai? Or Vietnamese?"

Ah, there she went, her face turning back to her normal color. "Vietnamese. Yum. Let's go."

They walked the block off campus to the nearest hole in the wall with a good reputation for their rice vermicelli bowls. Once they'd placed their orders, Garr leaned his elbows on the table, moving his face closer to Lia's.

"I need to apologize."

Her head pulled back. "What? Why?"

"I was a jerk." She started to shake her head but he held up a hand to stop her. "I was. Yeah, I got busy with work last week, but that wasn't until a couple of days after our date. I have no game whatsoever, and I just wasn't sure..."

Lia's lips parted and a light of understanding grew in her eyes. "My singing." A twitch playing her mouth had him grinning.

"Well, that *was* an experience."

Her laughter was music, especially compared to her

singing. "That's one way to describe it."

"Bah," he flipped a hand up. "It endeared you to me even more."

Her laughter faded but her smile remained. "It did?"

"Yeah." He reached across the table and took her hand in his. Her skin, warm and soft, felt so good against his. "It did."

"Oh. Well, then. Should I serenade you right now?" Lia took a deep breath and opened her mouth.

"Ah!" He practically flew across the table to clap a hand over her mouth. Laughter shone in her eyes. "Uh, maybe not right now."

A puff of breath against his hand warmed him. He gently lifted it off her face to find her laughing. "Okay. Maybe not. But one day soon..."

Soon. He liked that. "Speaking of 'one day soon,'" he took a deep breath. "I would love to take you out again."

"You would?"

Heat flooded his body. Yeah, he would. "Very much."

"On a date?"

Garrison leaned further, bringing his face even closer to hers, and whispered. "On a lot of dates."

Lia bumped her nose against his. "I don't know about that."

He lifted a hand and cupped her cheek before whispering, "I triple-dog dare you." A little closer had his lips brushing hers.

As he leaned away, Lia's eyes remained cloessd, a smile playing the corner of her oh-so-kissable mouth. "Well, I can't turn down a triple-dog dare, can I?"

"Nope," he replied, and leaned toward her again, savoring every moment of their second kiss.

&pilogue

"I don't know if this is such a good idea, Tyler." Allegra's hand hovered over her stomach. Was she still sick from that virus? Lia peered closer at her new friend. Her skin almost glowed. And Tyler was being extremely gentle with her.

Was she...?

Warm arms wrapped around her waist from behind. Lia leaned back into Garr's embrace. "I can't believe we're doing this. Tyler might have too much influence over our lives."

Beside Garr, the accused snickered. "You're going to love this." He looked down at his wife. "You will too. And it's safe. I checked." He winked at Allegra, who just shook her head.

A woman called out several names. "And Hawk."

"That's us." Tyler pulled Allie's hand and walked toward the woman.

Garr and Lia followed. "My stomach is in knots. Are we sure about this?"

His fingers squeezed hers. "Uh, sure."

It wasn't so reassuring that his voice cracked.

They were led to seats on the other side of the platform. "Please buckle yourselves in. We'll be around to secure you in a moment. In the meantime, may I take your drink orders?"

Lia leaned toward Garr and whispered in his ear. "Would you judge me if I drank an entire bottle of wine?"

He laughed, the brat. Before he could reply, however, the man taking their orders spoke up. "I'm sorry, but we don't serve alcohol." He looked around the platform without walls and grinned. "For obvious reasons."

Mm-hm. Her boyfriend's friend was going to pay for daring them to join him and Allegra. And if Allie's expression was any indication, she was going to make Tyler's life miserable.

He deserved it.

"Ma'am? Your drink?"

"I don't know if drinking anything is a good idea. There's no bathroom and this is freaky, sooo..."

Garrison's shoulders shook, but he was smart enough to not vocalize his humor.

A few minutes saw their harnesses double-checked by the staff. The floor underneath them shook and a few diners gasped.

Lia refused to confirm nor deny that she was one of the gaspers.

It took a few minutes, but their wall-less dining room reached 164 feet in the sky. She was pretty sure her heart had stopped several times on the way up. Once they were at altitude, the chefs, secured by harnesses themselves, began preparing the gourmet meal.

She leaned across Garrison. "Allie, you okay?" Her friend looked a little gray.

"Oh, yeah. Fine. Totally fine."

"Hey Lia."

She looked past Allegra at Tyler. "Yep?"

"I hear they might do karaoke if we ask."

And that, dear friends, is how Garrison McGarville died. Lia slid her gaze to the man she thought she might have been falling in love with. Hm. She'd have to re-examine herself.

He grinned and leaned forward, his lips touching hers and melting her into a puddle.

Re-examine what again? Nah. She was good.

The End

Acknowledgments

As always, first and foremost, Jesus gets all the praise. I'm thankful not only for His salvation, daily mercies, love, and grace, but for this gifting He's given me and the community of creatives He's provided as I make this writing journey, including the sweet ladies in this collection.

To my real-life "Garrison." Mark, this is my military retirement gift to you: a hero *completely* based on you. HAHAHA!!!! I know you love it. Just as much as you love *Goonies*. (You guys. For real. He has the shirt described in this novella. #helloinspiration)

My kids, Ethan, Van, and Elliette. You rock. And to the newest addition to our family, Ashlyn. Thank you for loving Ethan so much. Maybe one day I'll fictionalize your love story.

Toni Shiloh, *thank you so much* for the title! And your invaluable input on covers. You seriously rock, sweet friend. Love!!

Carol Moncado and Bethany Turner, what in *the* world would I have done without you?! You two saved me...or at least this story. Thank you.

The ladies in the *Once Upon a Laugh* novella collection: Krista, Pepper, Betsy, Christina, Heather, Laurie, and Jessica. Thank you for bringing such a newbie into this incredible and experienced group, for taking a chance on me, and for your offers of help and support as I wanted to rip out each hair on my head one-by-one.

And you, dear reader...thank you.

PS – I'm super proud of myself for keeping this so short—you should see *Count Me In*'s acknowledgements. Whoops.

If you enjoyed Garrison and Lia's story, I would so appreciate if it you head over to Amazon and Goodreads to leave a review! Even if it's just one very short sentence like "I loved it!" You'd make this author cry. A good cry. Though I warn you, I'm an ugly crier.

Mikal Dawn is an inspirational romance author, wedding enthusiast, and proud military wife. By day, she works as an administrative assistant for an international ministry organization, serves in her church's library, runs her kids to football, Tae Kwon Do, and figure skating, and drinks lots of coffee. By night, she pulls her hair out, wrestling with characters and muttering under her breath as she attempts to write. And drinks lots of coffee. When she isn't writing about faith, fun, and forever, she is obsessively scouring Pinterest (with coffee in hand, of course!) for wedding ideas for her characters.

Originally from Vancouver, Canada, Mikal now lives in Oklahoma with her husband, Mark, two of their three children, and one ferocious feline who can often be found taking over her Instagram account.

CPSIA information can be obtained
at www.ICGtesting.com
Printed in the USA
LVHW110602080722
722994LV00004B/527